THE RIVER WILD

THE RIVER WILD

A THRILLER

DENIS O'NEILL

Skyhorse Publishing

Skyhorse Publishing books may be purchased in bulk at special discounts for sales promotion, corporate gifts, fund-raising, or educational purposes. Special editions can also be created to specifications. For details, contact the Special Sales Department, Skyhorse Publishing, 307 West 36th Street, 11th Floor, New York, NY 10018 or info@skyhorsepublishing.com.

Skyhorse® and Skyhorse Publishing® are registered trademarks of Skyhorse Publishing, Inc.®, a Delaware corporation.

Visit our website at www.skyhorsepublishing.com.

10 9 8 7 6 5 4 3 2 1

Library of Congress Cataloging-in-Publication Data is available on file.

Cover design by Erin Seaward-Hiatt

Print ISBN: 978-1-5107-1598-1
Ebook ISBN: 978-1-5107-1599-8

Printed in the United States of America

To the Montana Team—
For all the friendship and adventures,
past and pending.

1

Forty-eight-year-old Mary Walsh pulled her 2009 red Ford sedan up to Debbie's Gas & Wash, do-it-yourself car wash, in Deer Lodge, Montana. She had moved to Deer Lodge, population three thousand, from the big city of Bozeman after a bad divorce. She had long since accepted the presence of the state prison a couple miles west of town—happier for the employment it provided her neighbors than she was worried about the inmates it housed. That peace of mind allowed her to venture out at all times of day, unafraid to walk along the banks of the Clark Fork River that meandered through town. She embraced the community's diminished pulse, and her middle school science class embraced her. She had been disappointed in love, but she hadn't given up. Life rewarded her persistence with a sixty-year-old man who was as gentle and solicitous as her ex was intemperate.

This relationship is what brought her to the car wash on this early June evening in a slightly flustered state. Friday was date night. She had a dinner date with *you-know-who*, and she wanted her car to be as scrubbed as she was. She glanced nervously at her watch; *not enough time*. She backed up, started to drive off, and then stepped on the brake, torn by indecision. The car herky-jerked to a stop. Mary climbed out of the driver's seat and took a look at the mud-splattered chassis. She looked at the sign that advertised THE BEST SHINE IN MONTANA. She consulted her watch again, climbed back into her car, and approached the security arm of the wash shed a second time.

Mary fed two dollars into the machine. Classical music seeped out of her open window. She waited until the security arm lifted in front of her, then rolled up her driver's window and eased her front tires onto the guide tracks. She turned the ignition off but left the battery on so she could hear the stirring end of the symphonic composition. She turned the volume up. As her car lurched forward, she reached for her purse and fished in its contents for lipstick. Distracted, she did not see the man ease out from behind one side of the wash shed, glance around shifty-eyed like a cartoon character up to no good, and slink up to her back door.

Because of the music and because he closed the door softly, she didn't hear him climb in either. He was wearing gray cotton drawstring pants and a gray cotton top with numbers stenciled on a lone pocket and the larger black letters MSCI splashed across the chest.

As the car moved deeper into the shed, water pissed down, and giant pompom cleaners descended on the roof and sides. Liquid soap engulfed the shell of the car in a cocoon of cleansing froth. Inside, Mary leaned forward as a new set of soapy pompoms attacked her windshield. She looked at her face in the mirror, turning it one way, then another, trying for a more favorable angle. Resigned to the homely appearance that had stared back from every mirror she had ever looked into, she started to apply lipstick, happy to accept the reality of life as a progression of small victories. She was a teacher of science, after all, not mythology.

Even if she had glanced out her side window, the mousse of soap suds would have prevented her from seeing a second escapee from the Montana State Prison in signature gray drawstring pants slink along the interior edge of the corrugated steel shed, keeping pace with the car until the pompom nearest him retracted upward. He was larger than the first man, with an oddly shaped torso that looked like Magritte's surreal sculpture. The wide lower body gave way to a size-smaller middle section, which gave way to a size-smaller head. He reached for the handle of the back door nearest him and climbed into the slow-moving vehicle. As the door clinked shut, the rinse cycle opened up with a mighty, multinozzle assault. Water ricocheted off metal and glass with a percussive din.

Minutes later, the front grill and hood of the car emerged to the softer acoustic of hundreds of cloth tendrils swabbing the car dry. Slowly, the windshield emerged free and clear. Mary Walsh was no longer driving. The first man to climb into her car was Deke, by name. His partner in crime, Terry, sat shotgun, his pasty white face also visible through the windshield. Both men were in their thirties.

Deke started the engine when the car's rear tires cleared the guide track. He aimed the Ford out of Debbie's Gas & Wash and into light traffic on Main Street. Mt. Powell loomed in the distance, its top still snow-covered in late June. Mary's face stared up from the backseat floor, her body grotesquely stuffed into the narrow space. A smear of lipstick angled up from the corner of her mouth, marking the moment her neck was broken. Her eyes were frozen in an expression somewhere between horror and surprise. The rousing conclusion of the symphony added acoustic punctuation to this latest subtraction from life in Deer Lodge, Montana.

Deke poked at the radio buttons.

"Can't drive to this shit." He hit the buttons four or five times until an up-tempo country song shitkicked out the speaker. Deke started to laugh. "I think we just redefined *clean* getaway!"

Terry took a moment to absorb the joke. Information reached his brain Brontosaurus-style—slow boat from the tail up to the tiny head. He smiled in time. . . . *Got it!*, he thought, while bobbing his noggin to the beat. Behind him, Mary's head jiggled slightly as the car gathered speed.

2

Rhododendrons the size of dumpsters formed a welcoming wreath around Tom and Gail MacDonald's black-shuttered gray Victorian in Brookline Village. A lovers' swing hung from the rafters of a beckoning front porch. In warm weather it was a perfect place to sit and sip summer drinks and watch fireflies and passersby and contemplate man's place in the greater scheme of things. Tom, an architect, had never developed his theory into a full-blown article, but he had told Gail on many occasions that he was pretty sure you could trace the decline of civility in society to the demise of front porches in modern architecture . . . specifically the social interaction with neighbors and foot traffic they provided. A wind chime tied to a wisteria vine tinkled in a sudden breeze. It was joined by the sound of a knife on glass through an open window.

In the dining room, Jim Ladage—a forty-something Wellesley banker sliding into corporate softness—rapped his butter knife against his wine glass once more, and set it down, having secured the desired silence. Jim was a family friend and occasional squash partner of Tom. He lifted his glass to Gail at her end of the table. Gail wore blue jeans and an embroidered, Western-style white shirt, sleeves rolled up to reveal strong, tan forearms. Her sandy-colored, shoulder-length hair poked out of a hastily gathered bun secured by a blue rubber band.

"First a toast to the chef," Jim said. "No, actually . . . first a toast to the chef's *father,* who taught her how to fly fish in the great state of Montana when she was a young girl and also put oars in her hands at a very early age. We are thankful for all the grateful and ungrateful sports you guided down all those Big Sky rivers . . . for all the fishy and fishless days . . . for all the time applied to learning your craft so that when the bar beckoned and the bright lights of Boston led you away from home, the fishing fires were only banked and never extinguished . . . and the fishing clients you always dreamed of would some day miraculously appear in your very dining room." He flung out his arms, like a gymnast after sticking a landing. "Thanks to you, next time we meet we'll be gathered around a campfire two thousand miles from Boston, looking at Montana stars, listening to the River Wild, eating pan-blackened trout."

"Oh Christ, the kiss of death." Gail sighed. "Haven't I taught you *anything*? You *never* pull out the camera before the fish is in the boat, and you *never* eat the fish before you catch it. We're sunk."

Jim wagged a defiant finger. "That's where you're wrong, because for the first time *ever* we'll be packing our own secret weapon . . ." He swung his glass toward Tom, who was slumped in his chair at his end of the table, visibly bored. Tom wore a blue work shirt and khakis. His long, salt-and-pepper hair was slicked back behind his ears. He was many years removed from his boarding school days, but taking the boy out of the prep school did not take the prep school out of the boy. Not even four years at Dartmouth could do that.

"*Tom*—the city boy, bon vivant, and long-standing member of Red Sox Nation, who once upon a time had the good sense to ask out the country girl his firm hired to do their legal shenanigans . . . had the *better sense* to make her *his* partner . . . and ended up forging the unlikely East/West, indoor/outdoor, always . . . um, *entertaining* . . . pairing seated at this table, this evening."

Jim was a little drunk. He paused to wet his whistle and ponder the wisdom of describing further a marriage well known to be fragile, sometimes volatile—a blend of passion and peril that, like many marriages, worked slightly better than it didn't.

His wife glared at him from her seat. In case her subtle recommendation was in doubt, she swiped her fingers across her neck in the universal signal to abort. Jim didn't have to step out of the batter's box to read the sign. "To Tom—a first-time fisherman and a very brave man. The trout won't stand a chance."

Peter Thoma, seated across from Jim, lifted his glass to Tom.

"Here, here."

"No, no," Jim said, "*There, there!* . . . To the River Wild. And even though we get a day's head start, Peter and I promise we'll leave a few trout."

Gail covered her eyes in mock despair—trout gods being tangible deities in her experience. The muzzle of her golden retriever, Maggie, angled up between her knees. Gail discretely transferred a discarded chew of rib eye fat from her plate to Maggie's mouth. Mission accomplished, muzzle slipped from sight. Peter and Jim sipped their wine in sync. Their nonfishing wives, seated beside them, smiled at each other, familiar with the bluster of husbands whose rigorous training at an Orvis weekend fly fishing school had instilled in them confidence disproportionate to competence. No matter. They were happy for their husbands to share a piece of male bonding that gave them—the women—leverage for trips and purchases of their own. Time apart was gift enough, but leverage being leverage, it was a sentiment ever unspoken.

Peter and Jim finished their Malbec with gusto, practically chafing to get on the river. Gail took a sip of wine and eyed Tom over the top of her wine glass. Tom returned her semi-critical look with a polite sip and a sarcastic smile. He raised his glass to his wife.

** ** **

Gail stood at the sink, washing dishes—glass of wine within reach—sleeves now pushed above her elbows. Gail was all about efficiency—a seed first planted on family camping trips, reinforced on hundreds of guided floats. There was a right way of doing things, and every other way. The goal was to know, or find the right way, or at least one right way. Life was murky enough; clarity in logistics made living it a little less murky.

Tom backed through the swinging door with a handful of dishes and placed them on the counter to Gail's left. She sighed and shifted the pile to her right.

"Tom, I've told you a hundred times—" She turned to add a visual to her complaint, but Tom had retreated to the dining room. The kitchen door was swinging back and forth.

In the dining room, Tom considered an architectural model on the sideboard. He nudged it closer to a vase of cut lilacs then angled it differently, as if siting the vacation house in its landscape. He reflected on the rearrangement for a moment, then shifted the smaller, stand-alone cardboard studio from one corner of the house to another, moving it closer to the lilacs. Satisfied, he collected the remaining wine glasses from the dining room table, blew out the candles, and took a deep breath, anticipating confrontation.

Gail was waiting for him, butt to the sink, arms folded. "You're going to hate this trip, aren't you?"

"I'm going, aren't I?" He made a point of placing the wine glasses to the left of the sink.

"The question is, are you going to make it miserable for everyone else? Because if you are, I'd rather not go."

"Dishes to the left, dishes to the right . . . stand up, sit down, fight, fight, fight!" He shook his head, "Good old Gail," he pumped a fist: "Not always right, but never in doubt."

"That's right, Tom! Thank God someone around here can make a decision . . . take charge."

"Ah yes . . . *the wearing of the pants.*" Tom glared at Gail. "Is that what its come to after fourteen years of marriage?! Who wears the pants? Let me count the ways: real men ride rafts down rivers. Real men climb cliffs and swim rapids. Real men—"

"Take *real* vacations with their families!" Gail stepped closer, aggressively. "Think about someone other than themselves and their precious models."

Tom simmered for as long as he could. "I pull my oar around here, and you goddamn know it!"

Gail smiled sarcastically. "At least the metaphor's a start. How about the real thing? Your son wants to go fishing. Is it too much to ask? You take him to Fenway. Why not Montana?"

Roarke appeared in the doorway behind his father, unseen by either parent. An only child, he was slight of build, with unkempt, sandy hair. He was thirteen, looked eleven, and sometimes spoke like an older teen—a condition brought on by his parents' early decision to forsake babysitters for the most part and include him in many of their adult gatherings. The upshot was a boy who still loved his dog even as he navigated grownup behavior and age-appropriate social media. Tonight had been an exception— a hall pass from a dinner party plump with trip logistics. At the moment, he had one hand rested on Maggie's head, the other held an iPhone connected to a headset slung around his neck. The sadness in his eyes revealed a child who had seen and heard too many fights.

"So where are we going?!" Tom hissed. "Fishing! With *our* son, and *your* friends to *your* old river to do something *you* love to do." He slow-clapped. "Another win for the prosecution."

"Poor Tom. Forced to spend a week in one of the most beautiful places on earth. Don't you want *your* son to see one surface without graffiti?"

"I guess I better go split a cord of wood before bed."

He turned. The sight of Roarke stopped him in his tracks. The boy's face shimmered with hurt and sadness. He blinked away tears. He wished he were older—older people seemed better able to deal with anger and disagreement and arrive at another place: compromise or resignation. Except when the older people were your own parents—then it just sucked, because they fought like kids on the playground, flailing away, missing as often as they connected, determined to stay on their feet no matter what. He slid his headphones over his ears. Hear no evil was the immediate goal, but Roarke knew his gesture also signaled disapproval. Point made, he turned and walked away.

** ** **

Gail sat on Roarke's bed in his dark bedroom. Roarke lay face to face with Maggie, with his back to his mother, his headset in place. Gail rubbed his back and shoulders for a while, rehearsing in her head what she wanted to say. She tapped him on his shoulder. He mustered a half look. She held up a finger—to request one minute *to talk*—then gestured for him to remove the headset. He shook his head:

No. She repeated the one minute promise, mouthed *Come on!* He shook his head to indicate he was not interested. Gail considered her options. She wiggled a hand into her jeans pocket and fished out a dollar bill. She tapped him on the shoulder again and offered him the buck.

"Usually, I pay you to be quiet," she said.

Roarke snatched the buck and slid the headphones off his ears. He turned onto his back and locked his hands under his head to reflect the difference between compliance and compliance with indifference.

"Okay," Gail said. "Do you know what subtext means?"

"No."

"It means sometimes when people say things, what they're saying isn't really what they're talking about. Does that make any sense?"

"No."

"Here's an example. When you came into the kitchen tonight and you heard Dad and me arguing about whether we wanted to go to Montana or not . . . specifically whether we, or he, wanted to take you . . . that wasn't what we were arguing about. We both love you and of course we can't wait to go to Montana with you."

"Tell that to Dad."

"Let me finish. Going to Montana with you wasn't what we were talking about. What we were talking about were things that have been going on for a long time, between us. Things that we say or do to each other that bugs one of us or the other, until we have this big bucket of bugs, and then your father puts the dishes down where he knows I don't like him to put the dishes down and it's one bug too many . . . and *boom*, all the bugs come out at once, but they aren't about going to Montana with you. Does that make any sense?"

"Why do you and Dad fight so much? You never used to fight this much. Do you still love each other?" Gail was grateful for the cover of darkness, so her hesitation wouldn't be so obvious.

"Of course we do," she said, "and more than that we love *you* more than anything."

"So why don't you just get rid of the bugs? Then you wouldn't fight." Gail blinked away a tear. She kissed Roarke on the forehead and lay down beside him. "I'd love to get rid of the bugs, honey. The river's a good place to do it. It always was for me when I guided. When I was younger. I found that being in nature helped de-bug me." Gail couldn't see Roarke's hopeful smile in the darkness.

"So let's go to the River Wild and get you debugged," he told her. "Make things simple, so that what you're talking about is the same thing as what you're talking about. Does that make sense?"

Gail hugged him tightly. "Yes."

3

Mary Walsh's red Ford sedan ended up in a stand of cottonwoods behind an old, weathered barn at the end of a dirt road not far from Belt, Montana—a smudge of a town not far from Great Falls. The town, which took its name from nearby Belt Butte was in the heart of Lewis and Clark National Forest. The barn sat behind an abandoned ranch house surrounded by rusting farm equipment. The car was not visible from the narrow county road that cut a dark, paved line through the great swaths of burnt-yellow hay fields surrounding the house, stretching as far as the eye could see. If you took the time to count the passing cars, on a busy morning you might use up all the fingers on both your hands. A pair of ravens sat on a branch above Mary Walsh's car, turning their heads one way, then another, staring curiously through a back window at a woman who held their gaze without blinking. Without moving.

** ** **

Deke and Terry, no longer dressed in their prison grays, stood atop a railroad bed in the middle of Little Belt Mountains, looking down a shale-coated slope to the River Wild, a mile or more below. Downstream, in the distance, the ribbon of blue was swallowed up by an endless vista of green mountains. All of it tucked beneath the big sky the state was known for.

Deke consulted a Montana road map, then folded it neatly and slid it in his jean pocket. He angled his head back and closed his eyes to take in the warm, early morning sun. He stretched out his arms. For a moment he looked like the Christ statue atop Rio de Janeiro's Corcovado. He pulled his arms in and twisted his torso left and right, to loosen up.

"Terry, I am never ever gonna let somebody lock me up in a cage again. Never. I will suck on the exhaust pipe of a mother-fuckin' RV before that happens." He took in the spectacular wilderness vista. "There she blows."

The vast remoteness and quiet of what he was seeing made Terry a little queasy. "I don't know that this is such a good idea, Deke. You know? Whole lot of nothing out there."

"Exactly why we're going," Deke explained. "'Least I am. Suit yourself." He leaped off the railroad bed onto the loose shale. He landed ten feet down the embankment, dislodging a handful of coaster-sized chips, regained his balance and bounded ten feet further down, like a mountain goat. His exuberant whoops accompanied the soft clattering of shale scattered by the force of each landing.

Terry watched him, his face filled with indecision.

He felt like the last jumper atop a stone quarry swimming hole. Backing out was not an option; it was just a matter of summoning the nerve. Overhead, a commercial jet carved its flight through a cloudless blue sky. Terry eyed it for a moment, wishing he were aboard. Then he took in the distant mountains—the place on the horizon where the blue of the River Wild seemed to vanish. He picked out Deke, growing smaller and smaller on the slope below.

"Fuck me." He took in and let out a breath, and jumped.

4

The inbound jet, originating in Boston, descended over the east fork of the Gallatin River and the surrounding fields of baled hay, and touched down at Gallatin Field, Bozeman, at the foot of the Bridger Mountains. Inside the plane, Gail peered out her window. She turned to Roarke, seated beside her, and squeezed his hand.

"Made it, honey. Home." Her face was radiant. Roarke smiled; he was used to his mother's mood-ring persona. She was not someone to bury the lead.

He angled his head to look past her, out the window. "Those are the Bridgers," Gail told him. "Named for a legendary trapper, scout, and mountain man, Jim Bridger. He was one of the first white guys to see the geysers in Yellowstone. Married a Native American woman. Loved the American West."

Roarke was as familiar with his mother's fondness for all things Montana as he was with his father's passion for the Red Sox. He had long since memorized all the lectures—

his and hers—and fine-tuned his lines. "How about you, Mom? What do you think about the West?" She wagged a playful finger in his face, *Don't sass me.*

** ** **

Maggie emerged from her travel crate at baggage claim, head bowed, tail wagging. Roarke grabbed her in an affectionate headlock. Maggie slobbered on him with grateful licks. Gail rubbed the dog's head. "Good girl, Mag. Honey, take her outside and find a patch of grass."

Later, they stuffed their luggage in a rented jeep and drove to a Livingston outfitter to collect the rest of their needed gear. Maggie savored the short drive with her nose angled out a backseat window. A handful of drift boats and rubber rafts were parked in a row behind the shop, each strapped to a trailer. A giant painted wood trout appeared to leap over the wood-shingled roof. Gail pulled out a notebook to check off the mound of rented gear: coolers, lanterns, propane stove, tent, sleeping bags, bungee cords, and other necessities.

Tom eyed the mound of gear. "Lotta stuff for three of us."

"Floating's a little like car camping," Gail told him, as she continued to check off her list. "If you don't have to carry it on your back, it's nicer to have it and not need it, then need it and not have it. Plus, where we're going, there are no 7-Elevens for fifty miles once we set out."

Gail aimed the car north from the Yellowstone River, east of Livingston. The route took them between the Bridgers to the west and the Crazy Mountains to the east. It was a country highway, mostly straight as an arrow, with undulating prairie land stretching away from the road and up to the lower slopes of the mountains. Traffic was minimal. Antelopes were visible in all directions.

Roarke and Maggie formed open window bookends in the back seat . . . each with a nose out the window . . . Roarke, headset in place, resting his head and shoulders on the doorframe. Tom sat back in the shotgun seat, happy for the wind on his face. Gail was in guide mode—a learned approach to life that coupled attention to logistics and details with an entertainment component that catered to the personalities of all aboard while providing storytelling backup when the weather turned bad and/or the fish went off the bite. She lectured as she drove, taking the wheel with one hand while gesturing with the other and alternating depending on which mountain range she was talking about. When she got to the good stuff, she'd flap an arm in Roarke's direction to require a lowering of the headset.

"So just to give you your bearings, we landed on the other side of the Bridgers. Those guys over there. And because of them, the Crazies, over there to the east, are drier and browner; the Bridgers cut off most of the moisture-bearing winds. Cool name, right? The Crazies. Want to know how they got their name? Funny you should ask, because I'm going to tell you. Supposedly there was a family named the Morgans, who stopped on the east flank of the Crazies . . . before they were the Crazies . . . en route to a new life in Oregon. The idea was to rest up before the final push west. Father, mother, two boys. This is maybe the mid-1800s. Anyway, one day, after the father didn't come home for lunch, the mother sent out her boys to find him. Next thing she hears these terrible screams. She grabs an axe and rushes into the woods. What she finds are five or six Blackfeet Indians slaughtering her family. Without stopping, she charges into their midst, wildly swinging the axe, killing four Indians and driving off the others."

Tom turned to Roarke in the back seat. "Sounds like something your mother would do."

"Bet your ass," Gail said. "The Ma Morgan Society. But she didn't save her family. And their deaths, they say, drove her crazy . . . and finally drove her to run off into the mountains, where she was never heard of again. But because of her story, from then on, they called the mountains the Crazies.

"How many times did you tell that story when you were driving clients to rivers?" asked Tom.

Gail laughed. "Enough to almost drive me crazy."

The jeep and trailered raft whooshed by an abandoned ranch house set back from the road. A bulldozer was plowing a road through the property. A sign on the highway read: RANCH LAND TO SUBDIVIDE. 40 ACRE RANCHETTES. NOTHING DOWN. $1250. PER MONTH.

Tom's inner architect rose up. "Build, build, build," he said. "Now we're talking."

Gail shook her head, disgusted. "They're chopping up this beautiful state."

Tom saw an opportunity to get her goat—a tactic they both favored and employed at will. "I know . . . how about one *gigantic* hamburger stand stretching from these mountains to those . . . " He sketched out the possible scope, swinging his arm in an arc. "We'll call it Big Sky Burger Boy." Gail resisted taking the bait. Her extended silence made Tom suddenly nervous, fearing a sudden, and predictable, Old Faithful eruption. He patted Gail on the thigh.

"Honey, c'mon. It's a joke. Gail . . . put the gun away. I'm kidding. It's just a joke."

"It's too true to be funny," she said icily.

** ** **

At sunset, the jeep slowed down to rattle across a cattle guard at a narrower road that angled off from the main road. A sign read: HOT SPRINGS CAMPGROUND, TWO MILES. Pavement soon gave way to dirt. When they crested a ridge, a river emerged in the distance—from this first vantage, it wound like a silver thread in a rolling green-and-brown landscape.

"There she blows," Gail pronounced softly, "the River Wild."

The first shapes and hues of a beautiful sunset began to form above it and the forested hills behind.

The campground held dozens of cars and rafts. Tents were pitched here and there, fires glowed in hibachi grills and under propane burners. Fellow rafters gathered in groups to chew on hamburgers and swap stories and hometown intel. Pre-trip conversation always glowed with high hopes and pent-up energy. Several boys cast spinners into the river. At this point, it was a sweet, easy-flowing body of water only twenty yards wide.

Gail found an open campsite to her liking and pulled

in. Roarke spilled out of his door, his young body stiff and coiled for release after a long car ride. Maggie bounded out after him.

Gail eased out of the driver's seat and corralled Roarke long enough to confiscate his headset. Tom grabbed a beer from a backseat cooler and joined her. Gail took in the kaleidoscope of colors now filling the sky . . . pinks and reds and salmon ribbons spreading atop the ridge behind the river like horizontal northern lights. It was a sight for sore eyes—the stained glass behind the altar in Gail's outdoor cathedral. Roarke and Maggie bounded past Tom and Gail and headed for the river's edge. Maggie was barking joyously. Gail walked to the river. She untied one sneaker, slid the half sock off her foot and dipped it in the water.

"Been gone twelve years," she said. "Too long. Would you look at that sky!"

A trout jumped out of the water, ten yards offshore.

"Look, a trout!" Roarke shouted.

Gail clutched Tom's arm affectionately. "Thanks for coming."

Tom handed her his bottle of beer. She drank deeply. Together they watched Roarke and Maggie patrol the bank. Maggie splashed into the shallows.

Roarke pointed to where another trout rose. "Get that fish, girl!"

Maggie barked and peered at the even flow of current, turning ever more silver in diminishing light.

Roarke pointed. "C'mon Maggie. You're a retriever. Get that trout." Maggie looked out at the unbroken surface, then up at Roarke, confused. She barked again.

"The trout, dummy. *There!*"

Gail smiled. Tom watched her study the river, practically mesmerized. "It's like a book for you, isn't it?"

"Yeah," she admitted, keeping her eyes on the water. "Moving, churned by currents, split by rocks, spun into eddies, scattered over shallow tail-outs. I love to read it . . . sort out the hydraulics, figure out where the fish are . . . or should be." She shrugged. "Comes naturally when you do it all your life."

Gail knew she had the "hunter instinct" all fishermen possess who grow up dunking worms for brookies and bullheads in small streams and ponds.

"I was always grateful for the fishing schools that got folks like Jim and Peter up and running," she said to Tom. "And got me clients. They could teach the knots and show them how to cast a decent line, but the one thing they *couldn't* teach is what lifelong fishermen learn when no one's watching: where the fish are going to be, when to change tactics, and when to move on when they're not there, or not biting."

"That, and don't let fishing get in the way of fishing. Rule number one." She handed the beer back to Tom. "It's important to me that Roarke learn about the outdoors. He may or may not be a fisherman; that's a hardwired thing. But I want him to appreciate this. There may be nothing here but 'ranchettes' ten years from now"—she gave Tom a look—"let alone Big Sky Burger Boy franchises."

"I couldn't agree more," Tom said. "Six nights sleeping on the ground and he'll appreciate just how great an invention the mattress is. Not to mention indoor plumbing." He wrapped an arm around Gail's shoulder. "It is beautiful."

"Yeah, just give it a chance." She looked downriver. "Just think, Peter and Jim are sitting around a campfire right now ten miles in." She felt only contentment. "It's such a peaceful river . . . here, anyway."

5

Jim and Peter had fished as much of the ten miles between the Hot Springs put-in and their campsite at Mile Ten as they could before darkness. They had a map Gail had given them, and two or three landmarks to look for as they drew closer, so as to not overshoot the site. The one-day head start was planned so they could get a full day's fishing out of one camp setup. Tomorrow they would wade fish up and down from the campground without having to break camp and repack the rafts; a bonanza of good water Gail had told them was worth pounding. Tom and Gail would pull in in the late afternoon. They would push off together the following morning.

By Mile Ten, the river had settled into the miniature Grand Canyon configuration it would embrace for the next fifty miles—a series of "S" turns with towering granite walls alternating on one side of the river, then the other. The River Wild had carved out its magnificent slalom course over many millennia. Snowmelt in the Lewis and

Clark National Forest unleashed a spring runoff that tumbled logs and boulders and gravel in the massive seasonal flow that ran as high as ten thousand cubic feet per second. It was the yearly scouring of the riverbed. Over time, as rivers do, the river had cut its way deeper into the granite bedding—the conveyor belt of abrasive materials acting like a giant, coarse sander. The trick for rafters was to book a trip when the runoff had subsided enough to bring clarity to the water and relative safety to the float . . . but not so low that the water warmed too much and the fish went off the bite . . . and not so low that you had to drag the raft over gravel bars at the end of the float.

In her guiding prime, on more than one occasion, Gail and a few of her more adventurous fellow guides would wait until the river was rip-roaring with runoff and then put in for the ride of their lives. It wasn't for the faint of heart or the inexperienced. Capsizing was common, the water was frigid with first snowmelt and cold spring nights. It was all churned up, too, making it all the harder to read the structure of any newly carved shoots and rapids. It was kind of a cross between bronc busting and river rafting. Once they even ran the Gauntlet—a class VI piece of white-water hell. It was Gail's favorite time of the year, client-free.

** ** **

Jim and Peter had set up their tent in fading light and collected firewood with their headlamps cinched in place. Because of the canyon walls, the darkness at the site felt like being in a three-hundred-foot-deep well. It was darkness that was almost tactile. Flames from their campfire, built in a stone ring, flickered in this black void—blues and reds in the bed of embers. It was warm and beckoning, especially after a day of rowing and fishing and standing in water. The sporadic crackles of the fire punctuated the constant *whoosh* of the river like bass notes and cymbal taps. It was a soundtrack that mesmerized and soothed better than any store-bought meditation sleep aid—an acoustic, once heard, that returned you time and again to the wilderness.

Jim and Peter had rib eyes and hash brown potatoes on board, a second bottle of Pinot Noir for a main fluid, and a bottle of twenty-four-year-old McCallan single malt whisky to help conjure memories gone by. They were sitting in low-to-the-ground camp chairs with back support, a requisite for campsite comfort no matter your age. The passage of time was always a topic on campouts and float trips, perhaps triggered by the river's timeless flow. Both men peered at the fire for long stretches, content with the company of silence.

"Tell you what," Jim said, after a long lull in conversation. "You know you're getting old when the drug of choice is Aleve, and the bodies you talk about are your own."

Peter laughed. Then said, "You hear that?"

Jim responded with "What?"

"Listen. I thought I heard something."

"Where?"

"Not sure."

Jim peered into the dark, unafraid. "Could be anything. But if it's a grizzly I want him to chew your bones first. I'm too full."

They listened hard for several moments.

"It's funny how your sense of hearing grows more acute when you lose your powers of sight at night," Peter said. "You ever notice that? Soon as the light goes out of the canyon, the river sounds louder. It must be your senses do that to compensate for what's lost. You know? Like there's some central sensory computer that constantly makes adjustments. That's why blind people have such a keen sense of touch." Jim angled his head back. A shooting star streaked across the ebony sky. "Rib eye in the hold," Peter said, "shooting stars putting on a show. Single malt. Fire. Beats work, buddy-boy."

Jim sighed, "Come get me Lord."

The sound of footsteps on dry leaves startled both men. They peered into the woods behind their pitched tent. Something was out there. Shadows seemed to move—at first, just dark motions in a black field. Then, one upright figure emerged, taking shape as it moved out of the woods and into the outer reaches of the light cast by the fire. A second figure followed behind. Jim and Peter sat up, alarmed. Peter grabbed his flashlight and aimed it in the direction of the approaching figures.

The light illuminated Deke and Terry—looking a little more haggard then when they leaped off the railroad tracks that morning. Their faces were smudged with dirt, their exposed forearms scratched. Deke stopped and held up a hand to shield his eyes. He waved in a disarming way.

"How you guys doin'? Saw your fire. We're camped

down the river a ways."Peter turned off his flashlight. Deke approached first. Moments later, Terry joined him at the fire's edge. Jim and Peter exchanged a wary look.

"Sorry if we spooked you," Deke said.

"Yeah, it's just us," Terry chimed in.

Jim and Peter rose from their chairs to face Deke and Terry across the fire.

"No, no, join us for a drink," Jim said. "Peter here had me thinking you were a bear."

Deke grinned. "That's good. A bear." He sized up Terry. "He's big enough, not me."

Then, suddenly concerned, he asked, "There's bears in these woods?"

"Mostly black bears," Jim said. "Maybe the odd Griz. Snakes are a bigger problem than bears, the way I understand it."

Worry washed over Terry's fleshy face. "*Snakes?*"

"Rattlers. Just watch where you step, and don't put your hand anywhere you can't see."

Terry looked like he was going to be sick.

Deke stuck out his hand. "Name's Deke. My buddy's Terry."

Peter shook his hand. "I'm Peter, this is Jim."

The men shook, kind of awkwardly, then Deke sank to his haunches and rubbed his hands together close to the flames. "Feels good, even in June."

"Got something to warm you from the inside out, if you're interested," Peter said. He held out the single malt.

"Don't mind if I do." Deke took a swig and examined the label. "That's the good stuff."

"No point in drinking the blended shit," Peter said. "Life's too short."

Deke gave that some thought. "Yeah," he slow-drawled. "No one gets out alive, right? So we try to burn brightly while we're here. You never know when your life can get snuffed out." He closed his fingers just inches in front of Jim's face. His eyes danced. A smile creased his face. He handed the bottle to Terry, who chugged it as if it were water. Jim and Peter exchanged a look, both of them thinking that something was just a little off.

Terry handed back the bottle. "Thanks."

"Why don't you warm up a bit before you head back to your camp," Jim said, gesturing toward the fire. "I didn't know there was another campsite around the bend. It doesn't show on my map."

"It's kind of an off-the-beaten-path site," Deke said. "A buddy told us about it."

Jim and Peter reclaimed their chairs. Deke and Terry settled on the ground.

"Jeez, it gets dark in these canyons," Deke said.

"Moon'll be up any time now," Peter told him.

"Good," Terry said, "I like it lighter."

"You fish today?" Jim asked.

"You bet," Terry said. "They sure got some big-ass bass in this river."

Jim glanced at Peter. "There's only trout in this stretch," he said.

Terry started to say something. Deke intervened. "Shit, yeah, but they're as big as bass. The ones we caught."

Terry held his hands a few feet apart. "Big as bass."

Peter whistled. "Nice fish."

Deke chuckled. "Well, they always get bigger around the campfire. Ain't that the truth."

"Amen," Jim said.

Peter pondered a friendly route to a gnawing concern. "You guys ever float this river before?"

"First time," Deke said.

Terry seconded, "Me, too."

"How about you?" Deke asked.

"Same as you, first time," Jim said. "We're meeting some friends tomorrow."

"They must be good to tackle this river."

Peter said, "Gail—the woman we're meeting—used to be a guide."

Deke nodded, "Bet she knows the river."

"Every bend and boulder, " Jim said, proudly. "Don't leave home without her."

Deke absorbed the information as he took in the immensity of the canyon. "Must be a comfort to you to have someone who knows the river so well."

Peter said happily "Especially when there's nothing between here and takeout but fifty miles of sheer walls, a few kick-ass rapids, and hungry trout."

Terry was visibly shaken. *"Fifty miles?"*

Terry's reaction did not go unnoticed by Jim and Peter, who shared a look. *What are these clowns doing on this river?* Jim thought.

"What're their names? Your friends," Deke asked.

"Gail and Tom," Jim told him. "And their son, Roarke. Why?"

"No particular reason," Deke half drawled in a friendly way. "Just nice to know who you're on the river with, I guess."

The men stared hard at the fire. The silence fueled suspicion.

Jim looked at Deke, whose face was bathed eerily in an orange wash. A bad feeling knotted his stomach. If he had been a mind reader, he would have known why. Deke was running the pros and cons in his mind, calculating the risk/reward of taking more lives. It was really just a matter of logistics.

He lifted his gaze from the embers and caught Jim studying him. Deke read his concern and smiled in a manufactured way that only deepened Jim's anxiety. Jim's sphincter tightened. His body tensed for the first time since he got off the river. The effects of the alcohol vanished. He felt instantly sober and uneasily focused. Which didn't help his nerves, because for the first time he confronted the realization that he was a man whose space had been invaded by something very dangerous, on a river with one way out. He shivered as if pierced by a chill wind. Jim felt like throwing up. And he probably would have, if he had seen the look that Deke gave Terry when they both lifted their gaze from the fire and their eyes casually met. The decision had been made.

6

At first light, river fog hung in shrouds over the glassy
River Wild at the Hot Springs campground. Tom and
Gail's tent, a stone's throw from the water, sparkled with
morning dew. A few folks were already up. Small plumes
of smoke rose up from fire rings in the riverside gathering of tents and trailers and vehicles. Rising time at camp-
grounds was always a staggered affair—affected by a range
of ingredients including the amount of alcohol consumed
the night before, the comfort of your air mattress, kids, and
the heat of the morning sun. The polite whispers of early
risers grew to a gentle murmur as they were joined by others, and the clanks of fry pans and coffee pots increased
incrementally. A blue heron patrolled the river shallows,
stepping gingerly, picking up each sinewy leg with care
and precision, head darting left and right on the lookout
for crawdads or minnows.

At first, the only sound from Tom and Gail's tent was
Tom's light snoring. Soon the sides of the tent were being

poked from within, like a creature trying to emerge from a cocoon. The front flap was unzipped. Gail's head emerged first, hair every which way, parting the two vertical flaps. She looked around at the new day. Roarke's head popped out just above hers, followed by Maggie.

Later, when the rising sun had burned off the river fog, the entire campground was up and about—tents being dismantled and stuffed into nylon sacks, trailers backing down the launch ramp to splash down rafts or drift boats, other rafts being carried to the water's edge, two porters to a side, breakfast plates and pots being cleaned. Gail, wearing shorts and wilderness sandals poured a kettle of water on their breakfast fire. The coals sizzled, threw up a cloud of white smoke. She stopped to pick up a hatchet stuck in a log.

At the river's edge, upstream from the camp site, Roarke and Maggie explored the shallow water. Tom emerged from the tent wearing wading shorts and a brand-new fishing vest with a price tag still stuck to a zipper. He spied Roarke and Maggie upstream and joined them.

"I've got a little present for you," he told Roarke. He handed him a Swiss Army knife. "Something to remember the trip by."

Roarke's eyes lit up. "It's a beauty, Dad. Thanks."

"They say it's a good thing to have in the woods."

Roarke turned the knife over in his hand, inspecting the seventeen different blades and tools. Tom smiled, visibly pleased. He rubbed Roarke's head, started to leave.

"Wait," Roarke called out.

Roarke opened the small scissors blade and snipped the price tag off his father's vest. "Better."

"I'm sorry about the other night," Tom told the boy. "I'm really happy to be here with you. Let's make sure we have a lot of fun, okay?" He held out an empty palm. Roarke slapped it.

Tom watched Gail back the jeep and trailer down the ramp. She hopped out and wiggled the raft off the trailer and into the river. She unclipped the bow line and clipped it onto the trailer frame.

"Tom, can you take the rig and park it, while I secure the raft?"

Tom climbed in and drove to a parking space. He made a final check of the jeep, grabbed a local newspaper from the front seat and waved it in Gail's direction. "Want me to bring the paper?"

Gail had removed her .22 handgun from its holster, wrapped it in a watertight oilskin and stuck it inside her day pack.

"Might come in handy starting a fire," she yelled up.

Tom folded the paper under his arm, locked the doors, and placed the keys on top of the front right tire for the shuttle driver to find.

Gail finished packing and cinching down their gear in the raft. She deftly swung herself over the side of the raft and placed her oars in their oarlocks. Roarke climbed into the stern seat holding his assembled fly rod. Tom held the raft from floating away.

"Where's Mags?" Gail asked.

Roarke placed two fingers in his mouth and uncorked an ear-piercing whistle. Maggie splashed downstream at the river's edge and leaped into the raft beside Roarke.

"I think we're good to go," Gail said. "Tom, just push us out of the shallows and into the current, then hop aboard." She slid the oars into place to help nudge them off the bottom.

Tom dropped the newspaper into the bottom of the raft and put a shoulder to the beached bow. The raft glided into the current. Tom splashed along with it, clinging to a canvas handle on one of the side tubes. Gail dipped her oars into the water.

She had plenty of depth. "We're good, Tom. Climb in anytime."

Gail held their position in the current. Tom swung a leg over the raft's taut rubber tube, but the current tugged the raft slightly downstream so that he hobbled on his planted leg for a moment before falling back with a splash. He slid the other leg back into the river. He was at a mid-thigh depth.

"Honey, get a little spring in your legs," Gail counseled.

"Sure—too bad white guys can't jump."

Roarke, grinning, pulled out his cell phone to video the next attempt. Tom gave him the evil eye, then measured the required leap. He gripped the canvas strap with both hands, and began to bounce in preparation for take-off.

Roarke offered vocal support from his seat, "Show 'em where you're from, Pops."

Tom sunk down a final time, then rose out of the water and flopped awkwardly over the rubber gunwale. He landed ungracefully in the bottom of the raft, drenching Roarke and Gail in the process. Tom picked himself up and settled into the stern seat. Gail removed a glob of weeds from her nose. Roarke was mud-splattered. He turned to his mother and wiped a hand across his face. Tom smiled, proud of the mini-mayhem he had caused. He made a point of staring directly into Roarke's phone. "*Brookline Village!* That's where I'm from."

Gail leaned into the oars and straightened the raft in the current. "All aboard. Leaving civilization." She mimicked a conductor's exaggerated cadence, "This raft stops at Two Falls . . . Bear Flats . . . Little Springs . . . and Canyon Gorge. All aboaaaaard!"

Gail took in the majestic rolling hills, the cloudless blue sky, the river bending ahead into wilderness. If she had looked down at the newspaper in the bottom of the boat now soaked by Tom's boarding maneuver, she would have seen a photograph of Deke and Terry, staring out from the front page in classic mug shot poses. Above their faces the headline and subhead read:

KILLERS ESCAPE FROM STATE PEN
DEER LODGE WOMAN MISSING

Each tug of the oar to position the boat sent another slosh of water onto the paper. The photos and news print grew ever more unreadable as the paper absorbed the water and the front page turned into a soggy blur.

7

The two-seat, single engine Cessna made graceful, ever widening circles in the air only a half mile above the rolling Montana landscape. It looked like a hawk gliding on updrafts, searching for a meal. The plane had a mission of its own, which explained its low altitude. Inside, the pilot scanned the rolling hayfields and tree-tufted rises, alternately looking out his side window and consulting a map to maintain his bearings and take stock of territory covered. Montana State Trooper Page Noel sat in the passenger seat, his eyes glued to binoculars. He trained them on dirt roads and copses of trees within reach of roads, abandoned barns, and ravines—any place a pair of escaped inmates might stash a getaway car if, in fact, they were the ones who had made Deer Lodge resident Mary Walsh inexplicably disappear en route to a Sunday dinner.

They flew over Holter Reservoir above Wolf Creek, then followed the Missouri River where it emerged below Holter Dam as a tailwater fishery. Page wanted to check the parking lots at various stops along the river where fishermen parked to wade fish or left cars to be shuttled. It would be a location where a parked car wouldn't be out of place, even over a period of days. And if the escapees knew anything about the shuttle system, it would be a place where a car could be easily stolen—its keys sitting atop a tire or inside the gas cap, awaiting a shuttle driver. He didn't want to spend much time because they were locations easily checked by ground vehicles, but it was worth a fly-over en route to more remote areas best surveyed by air.

Downstream of Great Falls, Page tapped the pilot on the shoulder and directed him to veer away from the river. He scanned the horizon with his binoculars. The little town of Belt was visible in the distance. Like many of Montana's rural communities, the town had to adapt to changing times to survive. Coal mining had given way to micro-brewing, a niche industry that helped keep five hundred or so folks on the census books. It didn't, however, keep any number of small ranchers from abandoning their hard-scrabble ranching lives. As in much of the American West, single-family ranches were an endangered species. There were too many of them for sale, and not enough buyers.

Page prided himself on being a thinking man's lawman, if that wasn't an oxymoron—a joke he told on himself. But for the same reason he wondered if the escapees knew about shuttle fishing and the vulnerability of cars left for hours with keys easily discovered. He also wondered if they had thought about the hardship towns littering the landscape and the probability that any number of abandoned ranches could harbor a getaway car and no one would know for months. He knew he could be overthinking things, but he had long ago decided to start with logic, just in case the other guys were playing the same game. For that reason alone, he checked out and wrote off several working ranches he saw in the distance, and directed the pilot to fly over one he saw at the end of a long dirt road with abandoned farm equipment in the front lawn and a barn missing half its siding.

As the plane approached the ranch, he lowered his binoculars to his lap and stared out his side window. The plane cruised overhead, a half-mile high. A dust devil kicked up between the barn and the stand of cottonwoods behind it, obscuring the trunk of Mary Walsh's red Ford. As the plane veered off, Page glimpsed a flash of reflected light coming from the cottonwoods—as if a beam of sun had ricocheted off something not made by nature. Page gave that some of his thinking-lawman consideration as the plane headed away from the ranch. He knew it could be anything—an old storm window, tractor windshield—but something bugged him. He tapped the pilot on the shoulder and made a circle with his finger: *do that again.* He plunged a finger down: *but go lower.*

A few minutes later, the dust devil had dissipated as the plane roared overhead only a hundred yards above the property. A pair of resident ravens flapped away from their cottonwood perch, scared off by the racket. Directly below them, the red trunk of Mary Walsh's Ford sedan poked out beneath the light-green canopies of the redwoods, clear as brown shoes beneath a black tuxedo.

** ** **

Detective Lieutenant Bobby Long of the Montana State Police set down the phone in his office in State Police regional headquarters in Great Falls. Bobby was an old rodeo rider with a bum knee and busted-up hands to prove it. Several bronzes of buckin' broncos were scattered here and there, remnants of long-ago victories. He had a robust gut that rested atop a belt buckle the size of a pork chop—yet another rodeo memento, this one for winning Livingston's annual Fourth of July Roundup Rodeo, one of the state's better-known rodeos. His complexion was perpetually red, no matter the season—not because of excessive alcohol consumption, although Bobby enjoyed his beer and Jack—but because a lifetime exposure to sun and wind had sandpapered him that way. He walked out of his office and stepped over to a huge wall map of Montana. His twenty-six-year-old assistant, William (Billy) Heston, a recent graduate of the State Police Academy, hovered at his elbow, devoted as a coonhound at his owner's feet. Billy had the build of a six-foot two-by-four and the face of a sapling. Compared to Bobby's boot-sole complexion, Billy's nearly whiskerless face was soft as corn silk. Billy and Bobby: the pair of them made for an odd set of law enforcement bookends. The lieutenant found Belt and the abandoned ranch.

He circled it with a red pen. He eyed the distance to Red Lodge—already circled—the scene of the breakout.

** ** **

Four trooper vehicles, a tow truck, and an ambulance filled the space between the abandoned ranch house and the stand

44

of cottonwoods. Forensic specialists took photographs and dusted for prints as the county coroner transferred a body bag from a gurney to the back of the ambulance. Four baying bloodhounds provided the main acoustic. Their trooper handlers gave them a noseful of the prison garb Terry and Deke had left behind when they abandoned the car.

Trooper Noel sat in a cruiser, door open, on the radio, providing his boss Bobby Long with an update. "We're dusting it now, Lieutenant. Probably a formality seeing as they left their prison duds behind, but better to confirm it's them."

"It's them," he heard the lieutenant say.

"The dogs got a pretty good scent," Noel continued. "I'm going to let 'em loose in a minute and see where we go. Hard to say how much of a head start they have, but we should get an idea where they're headed. Sons of bitches just clean snapped her neck, Lieutenant."

** ** **

Trooper Heston saw the lieutenant slowly hang up his desk phone. The lieutenant held his face in his hands for the longest time. Then he stood, walked around his desk, held Heston's gaze for a moment, and closed his office door. He heard a powerful *thump*, as if the lieutenant might have hit an inanimate object hard with a closed fist.

** ** **

Trooper Noel stepped out of his vehicle and pulled out a day pack from the trunk. He polished off a sixteen-ounce bottle of water, and put two more in his day pack. He checked his flashlight before putting it in the pack. He checked his revolver and ammunition. He unpacked a sniper rifle from its hard case, and grabbed two spare clips of ammunition. He clicked the Google Earth app on his cell phone, and marked his starting point. He slung the rifle over his shoulder and went over to the two troopers handling the hounds. "Got water and a weapon?"

"Ready to roll, sir." They, too, were wearing day packs, and boots built to navigate rough terrain. Revolvers were holstered at their waists.

"They snapped that woman's neck. You have any doubt they'll snap yours if they can?"

"No, sir."

"We don't know if they're armed or not."

"Understood, sir."

"We don't even know if they're still on foot."

"If they are, these dogs will find them."

"If we find them—and we will— keep that woman in mind. Okay?"

"Understood, sir."

"Let's go find 'em."

The troopers released the four hounds—with their sad eyes, dangly ears, loose gray skin, galloping paws the size of bagels—who immediately scrambled into the hayfield, baying at an ear-shattering pitch, happily unleashed.

** ** **

At dusk, the troopers and their hounds were standing close to where Deke and Terry stood before leaping toward the River Wild. The trooper handlers refreshed the dog's olfactory glands with a sniff of Terry and Deke's discarded prison clothes.

Two of the dogs headed back in the direction from where they had come. The other two headed up the rail line, trying to pick up a scent on the rails or railroad ties.

Trooper Noel was on the phone with the lieutenant. He eyed the rail line, which made a sharp bend where they had lost the scent. He gazed at the downslope of shale that fell off from one side of the tracks, angling down, down, down to the River Wild. The steepness of the pitch had triggered random mini-slides over time, making Deke and Terry's recent divots just two more gouges in an ever-changing landscape. He scanned the vast expanse of wilderness that filled the middle ground and far ground as far as the eye could see . . . to the river and beyond.

"You have the coordinates. You might check the rail schedule. If I were going to hop a freight, this is where I'd do it. There's a sharp bend, the train would have to slow down. I don't know if they looked at a map and picked out this spot . . . or stumbled onto it . . . but *if* my plan was to jump a train, this would be a good place to do it." He eyed the steep walled canyons that described the river's meandering course. "They could have headed for the river, but it doesn't make sense. You can see from here it'd take a hell of a cannonball to make it to the water . . . and there looks to be as much white water as not, which means it'd be all rapids if you survived the jump."

** ** **

Detective Lieutenant Long sat at his desk, looking at the crime scene photos of Mary Walsh. He gently brushed a finger across the lipstick smudge on her face—as if to correct a makeup mishap. He stared into her green eyes. Reluctantly, he set the photo aside and picked up mug shots of Deke and Terry. He was eye to eye with Deke when Trooper Heston walked in. "DA's office sent over the sentencing memorandas on the fugitives, Lieutenant. I'm going to do a little more digging and put together composite profiles."

Holding Deke's photographic gaze, Bobby Long said, in a monotone, "William Deakens Patterson. Thirty-eight. Born in Big Timber, Montana."

"You know him?" Billy asked.

"We go back," Bobby said. He eyed Mary's photograph. A sadness wearied his voice. "We all go back."

He dropped the photos on his desk and walked out to the wall map of Montana. The main rail line ran east and west across the top of the state, but there was another line that started in Billings to the southeast of Great Falls and ran northwest from there through Great Falls and Shelby en route to Canada, where it crossed the border at Sweet Grass. "Ain't exactly the size of Rhode Island, is it son?"

The young trooper took in the vast expanse to be searched. "You'll find them, Lieutenant."

Bobby Long snorted. He put his finger on the rail line as it passed through Great Falls. He traced it northwest, stopping where it intersected the main East–West line, then continued up to the Canadian border.

"Where would you go, son, if you were on the run?"

"Canada."

"I'll be goddamned. One plus one still equals two. Or in this case, *two* great minds equals *one* conclusion: Let's put every man we can around Sweet Grass. Cover the rail line and all the nearby roads that cross the border. Let's see if we can stay one step ahead of the sons of bitches." He paused for a moment. "Assuming they're stepping in that direction." He shot the young trooper a trademark grin forged by years of law enforcement red herrings and false leads. "Get me the schedule of all the recent rail traffic through Great Falls. Then get me someone I can talk to about this section of the track near Belt. Probably an engineer. Someone who's driven a train through there."

8

It wasn't far below the put-in at Hot Springs that the rolling ranch land and gentle hills gave way to the first signs of canyon country. A low cliff steered the river in a loose S turn—the first of hundreds to follow. Downstream, as far as the eye could see, hills gave way to ever taller mountains—like a wilderness graduation portrait, with the shorter members in the front row and the increasingly taller members in the rows behind. Patches of grassland in the near ground gave way to pure forest at the higher elevations.

The sun had driven the chill from the early morning air. Gail rowed in shorts and a tank top. Roarke, kneeling in the bow of the raft, braced his thighs against the converging tubes, to cast. He was bare-chested underneath a life jacket. Tom held down the stern. At the moment he was glaring at the birds nest he had turned his leader into. Loops of fly line were coiled on and around his legs and sandals. The monofilament leader was in his lap. His fly rod angled out one side of the raft, the butt section and reel at his feet.

Gail maneuvered the raft closer to a brushy cliff wall. "Roarke, put your fly close to the cliff. Looks fishy."

"Tell me what I'm fishing again, Mom?"

"Cheese," Gail said. "That's what we call any number of attractor patterns. Humpes, Wulffs, Coachmen, Stimulators . . . anything that looks like something good to eat . . . and doesn't imitate an exact fly."

Roarke's cast bounced off the cliff and dropped into the current six inches away from the rock.

"Perfect," Gail said. "Now take in your slack with your left hand . . . good. See how the fly's floating without drag. That's what you want. Makes it seem natural. The minute it starts to drag, you can recalibrate the float by mending your line, right? The way I showed you or by picking up the line and casting again." The fly floated along drag-free on top of the dark current, indicating water with depth. "It's really fun when the speed of the boat and the current are a match and you get a long, perfect float, like we're getting now. C'mon fish, eat it! You know you want it." Gail stared at the fly even as she back-rowed to keep the raft at a constant distance from the sheer wall. "Fish like to hang out there because they know the current pushes food from upstream against the wall, and there's also the chance of ants and beetles and other goodies getting blown off the wall into the water."

A trout inhaled the fly with a noisy splash.

"Strike him," Gail barked.

Roarke raised his rod tip, setting the hook. His rod tip immediately bobbed down, like a divining rod over a subterranean cavern of water. The fish leaped out of the water and crashed back. Roarke squealed.

"Nice rainbow," Gail told him. "Try to pick up the slack and get him on the reel."

Roarke fumbled with his line. "You're okay," Gail said, then mending her own line: "If you got him hooked well you are."

The line was puddled around the boy's feet, wedged between his body and the rubber tube.

"Keep the tension. That's it."

Tom finally freed his tangle, but paused to watch and cheer, "Show him where you're from, Roarke." Grinning, he said, "*Brookline!* That'll give him something to worry about."

Gail maneuvered the raft so that it floated perpendicular to the current, giving Roarke the opportunity to fight the fish head on.

"Tom, if you're untangled, bang the wall! Let's see if we can get our first double hook-up of the trip. Try by that log. Gotta be a trout there."

Tom peeled off some line and began to false cast toward the log, awkwardly. His cast overshot its mark and snagged on a branch. His reel began to scream as the snagged line pulled off the reel. Tom panicked. "What do I do?!"

The raft entered the shallower, tail-out section of the pool, then bumped into the predictably faster water below. Gail back-rowed like crazy, bracing her feet against the back of Roarke's tubular thwart, but the current was too strong. Roarke's trout bolted downstream through the rapids. "Mom," he shouted, "*What do I do?!*"

Gail couldn't help a laugh. She was back in the thick of things, just like the old guiding days—sitting in mission control once more . . . with *Houston, we have a problem*, incoming from multiple sources. It was her preferred briar patch.

She yelled to Roarke, "Let him run, honey, we'll fight him downstream."

Tom's drag was clicking crazily now as the line peeled off his reel at a faster rate. "That is one beautiful stick fish you have hooked," she told him, before calmly instructing, "Aim your rod tip at the fly and clamp the line to the rod with your hand. We'll get you a new fly below."

Tom did as he was told. His fly line tightened, its elasticity ran out . . . *Ping*, the leader snapped.

"Good, now reel in your line," she switched focus to Roarke. "Okay bow-man, I'm going to beach us and let you jump out and finish the fight. It'll be easier."

She rowed for slack water at the bottom of the rapid, opposite the cliff. When the raft ran aground, she pulled in her oars and vaulted the side tube to hold the raft in place. "Roarke, climb out, and fight him from the beach. Keep your tip up."

As soon as Roarke scrambled out of the raft, Maggie jumped out after him, splashing and bounding in the shallow water, barking joyfully. Tom reeled in his line and poked at the tippet where the fly used to be. Gail pulled the raft further onshore, grabbed her long-handled boat net, and quick-stepped over to Roarke to watch him try to land the fish. She took in the towering cliff, the green water sparkling in places where the sun pierced through the canopies of trees. She wore a goofy smile that might never fade. For her, this was the happiest kingdom on earth.

** ** **

Later, Roarke sat in the stern, hands folded behind his head, admiring the towering cliff. Gail sat in the bow, facing Tom, who had taken over the oars. Their rods were lashed to the side tube with bungee cords. The nose of the raft gently bumped against the granite wall, pushed there by the fast current at the head of the pool.

"No harm done," Gail coached, "but you can see how the current forces you against the wall . . . and why the fish might hang out there because all the food gets funneled that way, too. To pull yourself out a little bit, your instinct says to try to push forward on the oars and aim your nose out . . . but the hydraulics don't work that way. So back-oar your butt away from the obstacle . . . pull hard on the left only . . . that's it . . .then pull hard with both oars against the current."

Tom leaned into a few strokes, generating power from his feet and legs . . . up through his arms and shoulders . . . powering the raft away from the wall . . . his fists ending up tight to his chest.

"Look at you!" Gail said, grinning.

"You can take the boy out of the boat, but you can't take the boat out of the boy." Gail looked at him quizzically. "Which boat was that?"

"Pop's metal rowboat, Barco." Tom glanced over his shoulder to see where he was going. "We kept it in the marsh a few hundred yards from Long Island Sound. The estuary was filled with fiddler crabs and minnows and horseshoe crabs. We used to row it out into the Sound and catch flounder. A million years ago. Rowing's like riding a bike. Once you've done it, you don't forget how. You've just got to find where you left it. Same thing with camping, I imagine. Watch out, the call of the wild might transform me."

"It does that to all of us," Gail said, happily. "When you get far enough off, then you can straighten out your nose again and go with the flow . . . the secret of life, by the way."

Tom couldn't help but smile. If his wife's guide-bred need to instruct often rubbed him the wrong way, the content was usually well considered. Gail turned to survey the remaining stretch of water. She glimpsed Jim and Peter's raft on the beach, their tent set back from the water. "You can float for a bit right where you are Tom, then back-oar again to pull yourself out of the main current and get into the slack water that will deliver you to the camp site. Shoot to pull in just above Jim and Peter's raft."

Gail jumped out a few minutes later when Tom had successfully angled the raft ashore. "Good job, honey."

Tom gave her a look. "Just going with the flow."

Gail pulled the raft higher onto the sandy beach a few yards above their friends' raft. Maggie leaped onto the beach, followed by Roarke. Gail looked around—the site was empty. "Jim and Peter must be wade fishing downstream. The good news is they found the site. Free period," Gail said, "until we set up camp. Fish, swim, turn over rocks . . . whatever you want."

Roarke unfastened his lifejacket. "Time to catch more fish." He grabbed his rod, whistled for Maggie. "Where should I try first, Mom?" Gail surveyed the long pool.

"I'd start up at the head. Fish your way in. Make a few casts. Take a few steps downstream. Bang it off the wall. Gotta be trout stacked up all through there."

Tom fished in the cooler for a cold beer. He sat on the raft's warm, rubber gunwale studying the cliff, eyeing the eagle overhead, taking in the beauty of the venue. Gail watched him for a moment. He seemed visibly more relaxed, even after only a few hours on the river. She grinned, pleased.

"Tom . . . *relax!* You're too tense." Tom hoisted his beer in acknowledgment, without even turning to face her.

When Gail looked away from the river, Deke was standing ten feet in front of her. She stepped back, reflexively, spooked.

"Sorry," Deke said, "didn't mean to startle you." Terry emerged from a stand of trees and ambled up beside his partner. Gail studied the strangers. Both men were clean-shaven. Deke was wearing an LL Bean chamois shirt. Terry was wearing a plaid cotton shirt a couple sizes too small.

Deke waved in a friendly way, "Howdy. You must be Tom and Gail. At least the Gail part."

Maggie shimmied up beside Gail. Her golden fur stood on end. She growled. Deke knelt and held out a hand. "C'mon, what's that?"

Gail placed a hand on Maggie's head. "It's okay, girl."

Tom appeared beside Gail. He eyed Deke and Terry warily.

Deke stood. "Sorry again to give you a start. It's hard to hear above the sound of the river. I'm Deke. That's my buddy, Terry."

Terry waved. Deke extended his hand toward Tom. "You must be Tom."

Tom shook hands. "Tom MacDonald."

Gail put out her hand. "Gail."

Deke shook her hand. "Jim and Peter told us all about you."

Terry stepped forward and shook hands.

"Where are they," Gail asked, "off fishing?"

"Terrible thing happened last night," Deke said. "Jim was chopping firewood and cut himself with his hatchet. They had trouble stopping the bleeding, so Peter decided they'd better get him to a doctor, pronto. Rowing out was the best option . . . especially with a near-full moon to light the way."

"Is he okay?" Gail asked, concerned.

"He was looking at a bunch of stitches, and it was a nasty gash, but he should be fine. We wrapped it up pretty good. Truth is they were more worried about you. And Jim was pissed at himself for ruining Peter's trip. But we told 'em we were happy to stay behind and let you know what happened."

"Sorry if we held you up," Gail said.

Deke waved off her concern. "Fishing's good here. Truth is neither of us knows much about the woods. I think we got in a little over our heads."

"Jim said there were even bears," Terry said.

Gail smiled, "It's Montana . . ."

"They were going to let us tag along for a day or two, show us a few things about the river. Now . . ." He manufactured a look of anxiety.

"You can come with us if you like . . . that'd be okay, wouldn't it, Tom?"

"I don't want to seem ungrateful to you boys, but I was kind of looking forward to some time alone with my family."

"I understand," Deke said, looking hurt, nevertheless.

Gail bit her lip and shuffled her feet, embarrassed.

"I thought that was the point of the trip," Tom persisted. "You know. You're with friends by night, but on your own by day. I liked the sound of that."

Gail was torn. "I appreciate your wanting to do that, honey, but after what they did for Peter and Jim. Remember Clausewitz's first dictum about war: no battle plan survives first contact with the enemy"—she gestured to Deke and Terry—"not that you folks are the enemy, but you know what I mean. You gotta go with the flow. Especially when you're on the river."

Tom eyed Deke, then Terry. He didn't like the setup, but he didn't want to sound uncharitable. He glimpsed Roarke at the water's edge, staring at him—wondering if another family fight was in the offing. Tom offered a concessionary smile. "Why not. Incompetence loves company."

Gail made a conciliatory gesture. "Guess we'll make camp then and head out in the morning. We are never going to hear the end of this from Peter."

Deke said, "Let me help you with your gear."

He lifted the cooler from the raft and headed for the camp site. Terry grabbed a couple of waterproof duffels. "These go up, too?"

"Yes, thanks," Gail said. "Just leave them by the fire pit. I'll figure out where I want to pitch the tent."

Gail watched them until they were out of earshot. "What's the matter with you?!" she hissed at Tom.

"They're strangers! That's what's the matter with me. I thought this was *our* vacation?"

"What are we supposed to do? Of course we help them. It's the way of the river."

"Gail, you don't know a goddamn thing about those guys! Or what they do. They could be *republicans*."

"Oh please . . . just try to have a little fun, okay? Try. You were doing great."

"*Were* is right. Know why? Because is *is*. As in, is they strangers . . . or is they not? Yes, *they is!*" Tom gave her a look perfected over months of disharmony, the *don't-say -I-didn't-tell-you-so* look. He marched off, upstream, muttering to himself.

** ** **

Gail and Tom sat across from Deke and Terry—a blazing campfire between them, enveloped in a larger sphere of canyon darkness. The tiny beam of Roarke's headlamp was visible at the water's edge. He was cleaning dishes, assisted by Maggie, who peered at the dark water as if hypnotized. After a day of rowing and fishing and sun, Gail relished sitting and staring at a campfire. It was a primitive pleasure, connecting those in its glow all the way back to early man. Besides eating, it was one of the few continuous, shared ingredients linking modern times with cave dwellers. Staring at a campfire always did that for Gail . . . and for others, too, she realized, after watching it work its magic on dozens of clients on dozens of floats. It made you reflective. Made you consider your place in the scheme of things. Cajoled you into thinking from whence you came, and wondering where you were going. Beside the natural beauty of the landscape and the physical activities related to rowing and fishing, Gail loved the introspection that came with the territory. The spiritual involvement was as natural as the physical—a blended concoction she found intoxicating. It's why silence around a campfire was as savored as conversation, and conversation was welcomed in haphazard bursts.

"Jim told us you used to work the river for an outfitter," Deke said, puncturing one of those stretches of fire-crackling silence.

"A long time ago," Gail said. "Before I had to get serious and get a real job. Husband. Kid. *The full catastrophe!*" She laughed and placed her hand in Tom's. "Funny . . . everything in your life changes, but this place always stays the same."

She knocked her knuckles on a piece of firewood before tossing it on the fire. It landed in a small explosion of sparks. "At least, I hope it will. That's why I like it so much. Gets me back to basics."

"Too bad about Peter," Terry offered.

"I thought it was Jim who got cut?" Tom said.

"Did I say Peter?" Terry touched a finger to his temple as if to say, *I must be losing it.*

"You did," Tom said. His words kind of hung there, a little edge to them. "What do you guys do?"

"I'm sort of in between jobs," Deke said. "The economy being what it is, you know. Terry here—"

Tom interrupted him: "Why doesn't Terry tell us?"

"Not too much to tell," Terry said, suddenly a little self-conscious. "My folks were in the restaurant business. I move around a bit, waiting, managing, bartending . . . short order cooking . . . whatever I can find . . . a lot of seasonal jobs."

Tom looked at Deke and noticed he kind of tensed whenever Terry spoke. "How far you figure they had to go to row out? . . . Jim and Peter?"

"Good fifty miles," Gail said.

"How long would that take?" Deke asked.

"Depends how fast you row. Sixteen hours, maybe, if you rowed straight on through."

"Hell of a long day," Tom said.

"At least it's downstream," Gail said. "You can make progress even when you're resting."

"How many days you folks taking?" Deke asked.

"I'd take a month, if I had my way," Gail said. "But I'll settle for three more nights." She squeezed Tom's hand playfully. "Right, honey?"

"I'm more with Terry and my fellow architect Mies van der Rohe," Tom said, "Less is more."

Roarke emerged out of the darkness carrying a stack of dented aluminum dinner plates, some kindling, and the newspaper—now dried out—tucked under his arm.

Terry glimpsed his and Deke's mug shots on the front page. His face tensed. He nudged Deke and nodded toward the paper. Deke immediately sat up straight, eyes wide with alarm. Terry's hand crept toward the knife strapped to his shin . . . just in case.

"Roarke," Deke said, "can I take a look at the paper?"

"Sure."

He handed the paper to Deke and dropped the pile of kindling beside the fire pit. He sunk to his knees. "Okay to stoke the fire, Mom?"

"Yup, last call honey, before lights out."

Deke unfolded the paper and stared at his own image.

"Doubt you'll find anything interesting," Tom said. "Just the local rag. Yesterday's news to boot."

Deke calmly scanned the story for any actionable information. Terry leaned in for a glimpse. Deke crumpled the front page and tossed it into the fire. For a moment, his and Terry's wrinkled faces stared up from the coals.

"I don't know about everybody else," Gail said, stretching, "But I'm going to call it a night."

Deke's and Terry's photographs briefly glowed like a Chinese lantern before bursting into flames. They were gone.

9

Early morning light lay even in the canyon. Gail, wearing shorts, flip-flops, and a fleece, added a few sticks of tinder to the fire. She held back a towel draped around her neck, leaned in, and blew hard. The tinder caught fire. Gail angled some fatter kindling into the newborn fire, building a teepee around the flame. Satisfied she had the proper mix of draft and fuel, she balanced the charred camp grill on rocks above the growing flame. She settled the coffee pot on top.

She stood and surveyed the site: two rafts beached, two tents, rigged fly rods safely bungee corded to small tree trunks. Mile Ten enveloped in stillness. She made her way to the water's edge. She stared upriver. A water ouzel skittered across the run below the rapids that fed into her long pool. A trout sipped at something in the foam line just below where the rapid dropped off into the deeper water. She shed her fleece and shorts and tossed them into a pile on the sand with her towel. She kicked off her sandals.

She liked being on an even footing with her surroundings: naked. She stepped into the water and couldn't help thinking—as she always did when she entered moving water— that she never stepped into the same river twice. She loved the philosophic incongruity that on a river what had gone past was also what lay ahead. Past and future naturally blended into all that ever really mattered—the present. It's why she loved being on the river: it never failed to stir deep thoughts, while demanding attention to mundane logistics. Off the river, the logistics often took hold and became an end in themselves, shorn of wonder.

She waded in to midthigh depth, then dove in. She pulled and kicked hard for five or ten strokes, then let the current sweep her down river. She drew a breath and slipped beneath the surface. She swam toward the slack water closer to shore, then rose to the surface once more and began to swim toward the top of the pool, just in from the current seam. When she reached the top of the pool, she paused to take in the dense stand of pine trees that stretched from the campsite upriver. She didn't see Terry's head poke out from behind one of the tree trunks when she dove under once more to shoot herself into the current.

Terry tracked Gail's pale body, ghostly against the river's dark-green hue. He sighed when she surfaced briefly, took a breath and sounded once more, her bottom rising briefly out of the water. He touched his groin. He was hard. He swallowed, mesmerized. Deke's hand, clamped hard on his shoulder, broke the reverie. Deke looked past Terry to where Gail now floated on her back—head aimed downstream—breasts and pubic hair visible.

Terry's eyes sparkled. "Only thing sweeter than pussy, is wet pussy."

Deke nodded for Terry to get back to the campsite. Terry looked longingly at Gail.

Deke gripped his shoulder harder. "Now. We need that view for at least a couple more days. Don't fuck it up."

Terry abruptly wheeled on Deke and grabbed his throat. He pushed the smaller man almost effortlessly against a pine. Then he used his uncommon strength to lift him off the ground. Deke's hands went to his throat, to try and loosen Terry's grip. His boots clawed the air for a purchase. Terry peered at him for a moment, like a scientist examining a pinned butterfly, then released his grip and walked off. Deke bent over, struggling to catch his breath. It came in short, bunched wheezes.

Twenty-five yards downriver, Gail, sensing something, abruptly gave up floating to tread water. She glanced upriver, at the stand of pines. She saw nothing but tree trunks.

** ** **

Roarke sat on a rock at the water's edge, his sandaled feet immersed in shallow water, his headset slung around his neck. The sun had risen high enough in the sky to angle over the canyon wall and brighten Roarke's half of the river. The deeper current that ran along the cliff was still in shadow. Gail lowered herself on a rock beside him. The river provided a lulling *whoosh*—a kind of melodic pad that was joined at times by the warble of a songbird or the shrill

cry of a raptor riding updrafts along the rim of the towering cliff. Gail eyed the headset and couldn't help a smile.
"Glad to see you're listening to the original soundtrack."

"It's peaceful," Roarke admitted. "It kind of sneaks up
on you."

"It makes me happy you feel that way," Gail told him.
"And once your ears fully adjust, you keep hearing different elements. A wild river like this really is the original symphony if you think about it. Slow in places, then
it builds a faster tempo, next, you're in this big percussive
rapids section that riles your blood and stirs your adrenaline, then it reaches a crescendo and spits you out into the
relief of deeper, quieter water. Beautiful, soothing strings,
maybe, that put you in a pensive mood, and you go along
with that for a while, happy for the relief until you turn a
bend and off you go again with the giddyup portion. That's
not even counting all the guest soloists: thunder, lightning,
wind, rain. All for free, too. As long as we keep it wild." She
poked Roarke with a gentle finger. "That means you, after
I'm gone."

"Not soon, right?"

Gail mussed his hair. "Right."

For a moment, they let the river run through them,
wash over them. "You're different out here than you are in
Boston, Mom."

"Ha!" Gail chirped, "my son, the shrink." After another
bout of silence. "It's true, I am. "

"I think Pop's even getting in the flow."

"It sneaks up on everybody."

Roarke peered at his mother. "How are your bugs?"

Gail laughed. "What bugs?!"

Roarke glanced back at the camp and saw Deke and Terry pouring coffee. "You think Deke and Terry are bugs?" Roarke asked.

Gail looked where Roarke was looking. "Nah. We're going to do exactly what we want to do—what we planned to do—and they'll probably just do their own thing once they get the hang of it."

She stood and angled her face to catch the sun. She squeezed her eyes shut and thrust out her arms, exuberantly.

Roarke smiled. "Relax, Mom, you're too tense."

A grin creased her sun-warmed face. "I have to remember you actually hear everything I say," Gail told him. "You don't always listen, but you hear."

10

Gail liked to describe Montana's seasons as, "Ten months of winter, and two months of company." The *company* component was true of the scenic, mountainous western portions of the state. Elsewhere, as in Sweet Grass and other prairie towns, it was more accurately "Ten months of winter, two months of barbecue."

Sweet Grass, population fifty-eight, sat on the forty-ninth parallel—the border between Canada and the United States defined by the terms of the Oregon Treaty of 1846. In time it became the place where two major routes—one rail, one highway (Interstate 15)—entered Alberta, Canada. It was the most heavily traveled port in Montana and the only commercial border crossing open twenty-four hours a day. There was no physical boundary here—water feature or mountain range—just a line in the arid soil that separated wind-swept prairie land to the north, from wind-swept prairie land to the south. Which isn't to say Sweet Grass didn't have its hometown celebrities—Earl Bascomb, the "father of modern rodeo," being one; Charles M. Russell, the well-known (though mostly in the nineteenth century) cowboy artist and sculptor, being the other; but if you happened to find yourself in Sweet Grass, Montana, chances were good you were passing through. Which is why the traffic was backed up for a mile at the border, matched by two hundred freight and grain cars that were stopped in their tracks within eyesight of the car snarl, its four-pack of engines sitting motionless at the border. Montana State Police Lieutenant Bobby Long suspected two fugitive suspects wanted for murder might also be trying to pass through. The sign at the Customs tolls said: WELCOME TO CANADA . . . BIENVENUE AU CANADA, but the welcome south of the border was hardly friendly. A half dozen heavily armed Montana state troopers, some with dogs, checked every driver's license, every trunk, RV, and truck making its way north into Canada. It didn't make for a happy gathering of summer travelers, something rookie trooper Billy Heston tried to take in stride as he made his way down the lineup of disgruntled drivers, holding a stack of mug shots of Deke and Terry, explaining the situation. It didn't help that it was ninety-five degrees on the sun-blasted sheet of concrete spread like an apron south of the actual border crossing.

Billy stepped up to a green Honda Odyssey whose roof rack bristled with camping gear, coolers, duffel bags, and spinning rods bungee-corded to the main lump of gear. The driver's window eased down as he leaned close. Husband and wife sat in the front seats looking a little worse for wear—a disposition well-known to survivors of summer road trips with the kids. The woman had little white dabs of bug bite cream on her face and sleeveless arms. The husband's nose was peeling. He was unshaven. There were three kids and two dogs in the back, more gear in the far back.

"Afternoon, folks," Trooper Heston said. Sweat streamed out from under his trooper's hat and down his face. "There's a manhunt under way for two fugitives. These are their pictures. We're making the public aware of this circumstance because they're considered armed and dangerous, but also to solicit your help should you have seen or come across either fugitive. These are for you to hold onto. He handed Terry's mugshot to the driver, who looked at it and handed it to his wife. Billy handed Deke's mugshot to the driver. The face of a seven-year-old, wide eyed and freckled beneath a buzz cut, poked between the front bucket seats. "What'd they do?" he asked hopefully, "kill someone?"

"Trevor!" his mother gasped.

"As a matter of fact, they're wanted for homicide," Billy said.

The boy wrinkled his nose. "Does that mean killing?"

"Unfortunately, yes," Trooper Heston told him. "Thank you for your patience. We have teams with dogs that will be following up. Obviously, don't stop to pick up strangers. And if you see or come across either of these men, do not interact with them yourselves, but please call the hotline number listed on the bottom of the mug shot. They may, or may not, be traveing together. "

Trevor couldn't believe his good fortune. "Cool!"

Billy tipped his hat politely and moved on to the next car. The squawk of car horns continued—some nearby, some hundreds of yards distant. Occasionally, patience prevailed and silence followed. Soon enough, a frustrated honk would unleash a chorus of collective disgruntlement. It added a layer of acoustic abrasion to an already over-heated situation. Heston smiled through clenched teeth at glaring faces and reminded himself what the lieutenant had told him: *You can't make an omelet without breaking eggs.* The lieutenant was full of no-nonsense sayings and literary references collected over his sixty-one years of mostly hard living. Some were time-tried truths: *A stitch in time saves nine . . . No time like the present*, applicable to day-to-day living and general law enforcement logistics. Others, such as: *He that tastes women, ruin meets,* were a little less relatable to the general public.

As he moved from car to car, from pissed-off driver to pissed-off driver, the young trooper dredged up the ones that had a bearing on persistence. *The harder I work, the luckier I get,* came to mind. Billy liked to run through them in his head not only because some of them were actually useful, but because reciting them to the lieutenant at appropriate junctures seemed the best way to express his admiration for his mentor.

Trooper Page Noel was on bloodhound duty once more, just a "bay" away from Billy and the long line of traffic. Accompanied by a representative of the rail line, he oversaw teams of troopers and dogs that made their way from freight car to freight car, checking for unwanted passengers. It was tedious work in the hot sun—the unrefrigerated cars poured out blasts of even hotter air when they were clanged open. The symphony of honking horns and baying bloodhounds was joined by the new acoustic of a State Police helicopter clattering overhead, close to the ground, heading west—tracking the forty-ninth parallel for any suspicious foot traffic. It wasn't *Appalachian Spring*, but to the fifty-eight residents of Sweet Grass it was a tune they had heard before—the price of marking a border crossing. Below the chopper, miles from Sweet Grass, a phalanx of heavily armed troopers and other law enforcement personnel marched a yard apart, combing the landscape for any signs of the escapees, sector by sector. It was a grueling assignment under a blazing sun across uneven terrain, but it was boots on the ground—the foundation of textbook manhunt procedure.

** ** **

Warden Leroy Hesse ushered Bobby Long into his office on the sixty-eight-acre compound of the Montana State Prison, three miles outside of Deer Lodge. The prison held fifteen hundred inmates in a facility designed to handle maximum-, medium-, and minimum-risk prisoners. Before people came here to be incarcerated, the earliest visitors to the area were lured by the relatively pleasant weather in the protected valley. The same was true for the local deer population, which preferred the warmer climes to the colder temperatures in the surrounding high country, as well as the appeal of a natural salt lick produced by a geologic formation known as Warm Springs Mound.

Neither the salt nor the weather brought Long to the area, but some early ranch hand work here had taught him how to rope and ride. Later, he had delivered many a prisoner to the Big House as a young trooper. Warden Hesse was an acquaintance from his rodeo days—a former ranch hand himself, who'd decided babysitting hard cases was easier than delivering breached calves on frigid winter nights.

Bobby Long and Leroy Hesse shook hands warmly and swapped brief hunting and fishing conquests before getting to the heart of the matter: the early and unauthorized release of two maximum security inmates.

"Anything new?" the warden asked.

Bobby Long shook his head. "Not yet. Anybody hear anything in the yard?"

"No one who's talking. Deke was the big man on campus. Equally feared and revered." The warden hit his intercom. "Bring in the prisoner." Then he said to Long, "There is one new development."

A burly female marshall escorted a woman into the office and steered her into the empty seat beside Trooper Long. She wore a tan state corrections jumpsuit. Her hands were cuffed in front of her. She was heavyset, with a doughy face, thinning hair, and horn-rimmed glasses. The marshall stood behind her.

"This is Roberta Burrows. She worked for many years in the food department, here at the facility. She took a shine to Deke going back a bit and helped smuggle him the tools he used to cut and saw his way out. She has confessed to having intimate relations with the prisoner. She was going to meet him with a car and drive him to safety, but she had second thoughts. When she heard about the murder of the school teacher, she turned herself in. We've told her any cooperation with law enforcement officials would be taken into consideration at her trial. Ms. Burrows, this is State Police Detective Lieutenant Bob Long. Lieutenant Long is heading up law enforcement pursuit of the fugitives."

Bob Long looked at her for a long moment. "Anything you say can and will be used against you in a court of law. Do you understand?"

"She's already waived her rights, Lieutenant."

"In writing?"

Warden Hesse held up a piece of paper.

"Ms. Burrows, we would like to capture these men before they can harm any more people. Tell me how you first met Deke Patterson, how you managed to smuggle them tools, and if they ever shared with you their destination after you met them with your car."

"Deke told me he loved me."

Trooper Long sighed. "I'm sure he did. Before we go further, may I tell you what he did to another woman in a car? Snapped her neck, clean. That could have been . . . no, *would have been* your neck if you had picked them up as planned. Do you understand that?"

Tears began to slide down Roberta Burrows's face.

"I tell you that because I also know William Deakens Patterson. He's a diagnosed sociopath. You saved one life—your own—when you abandoned your rendezvous with him. There might be something you can tell me that will save other lives. So think hard." Trooper Long offered a sympathetic smile. "*No time like the present*, Ms. Burrows."

Roberta Burrows rubbed a sleeve across her tear-streaked face. She took a deep breath, began to talk.

11

Camp was struck and the rafts packed an hour or so after breakfast. It was a leisurely start intended by Gail to let the river melt away the urban tempo they lugged to its banks, as well as to give Roarke and Tom time to fish good water before it was pounded by other fishermen.

Roarke sat at the oars of his raft, now bobbing in shallow water, held by Gail. Terry manned the oars in Jim and Peter's raft, with Deke holding the nose. Tom, farther inland, cupped a hand to his mouth, shouted: "Maggie! C'mon girl!! C'mon Mags!! Boat's leaving!" He turned to Roarke. "Give her the old two fingers."

Roarke let fly with an ear-piercing whistle. Everybody stared at the gentle upslope into the steeper canyon wall behind the campsite.

Maggie heard the shouts and the whistle and barked back. She was some fifty yards from the fire pit, out of view—halfway up a slope of scrub trees and fallen leaves. She was pawing like crazy at the ground. Dirt flew between her legs as she beetled on, head down. More voices reached her, decidedly more angry in tone, making her more frantic. She barked and whined, stared toward her masters' voices . . . worried to be disobeying the command but caught up in what she figured to be a more important assignment.

On the beach, Tom was losing patience. He heard Maggie's barks and barked back: "Maggie get your ass down here!" He stepped closer to the barking. "Last chance Maggie!"

Sensing a parental meltdown, Roarke unleashed another mighty whistle and a high-pitched, "C'mon Mags! Good girl!" triggering renewed frantic barking from Maggie.

Tom turned to Gail. "I told you she'd be trouble in the woods." Exasperated, he headed toward the woods, muttering. He didn't see Deke and Terry's silent, anxious exchange.

Gail apologized to Deke with a look. Deke disarmed her concern. "Dogs will be dogs. Maybe I can help." He tugged the nose of the raft onshore and hurried after Tom.

Maggie, meanwhile, had her jaws latched onto something in the ground. She pulled with all her might, repositioning her hind legs for better leverage, slipping on the loose dirt, shaking her head as dogs do when they don't want to give up a bone or chew toy, growling with frustration.

Deke looked back to make sure he was out of sight of the rafters before extracting his knife from his pocket and cupping the blade in his palm. Tom had stopped to catch his breath on the slope and try to retrieve Maggie without having to climb all the way up to where he saw her golden coat and flying dirt. "*Maggie!*" His voice was all anger. "Maggie," he shouted, "goddamnit, get down here!"

Maggie glimpsed Tom some twenty yards away, considered the anger in his voice, and abandoned her mission after a final tug. She bounded down the slope and slowed to a guilty, hunch-shouldered shimmying when she reached Tom. Tom grabbed her firmly by the collar and steered her down the path. "Bad girl, Maggie. Bad girl. Go!" Maggie quickened her pace when Tom relinquished his grip and bounded past Deke, now only a few paces in front of Tom. His proximity gave Tom a start. He shook his head as he brushed past Deke. "Goddamn dog. Maybe a bear will get her."

Deke watched him descend, then peered uphill toward where Maggie had been digging. His view was obstructed by the angle of the slope, although he could see scattered fresh dirt. He returned his knife to his pocket and headed back to the river. He knew what Maggie was on to, even if he couldn't see the results of her excavation. It didn't matter now. It mattered less to Jim, whose bare forearm angled grotesquely out of the shallow grave, a single, bloody finger pointing ominously downstream.

Maggie was seated next to Roarke on the rower's seat when Deke marched up and shoved his and Terry's raft into deeper water. He climbed into the bow seat, facing Terry. The two rafts drifted slowly side by side in the slack water as Gail gave a brief rowing lesson to the fugitives. "Most of the time you want to keep the river in front of you. So, always bow first, and mostly what you're doing is steering. Let the current do the work. Okay? Nothing to it. Just follow us. The rougher rapids are days off." She turned to Roarke, who was at the oars. "Okay, honey, steer us into the main current."

Terry watched their raft center itself in the main current and glide downriver with increasing speed. He dipped his oars to follow suit. After a few strokes, they too were in the main current. The raft began to speed up. Terry looked as comfortable as a kid on a bike taking his first unassisted pedal. Deke smiled. "Don't forget, there's nothing to it."

** ** **

A couple miles downriver, Gail took the oars to steer them through a moderate rapid. Roarke and Maggie were in the bow, hunkered in, Roarke's knees on the floor of the raft.

"Hold on!" Gail commanded.

Roarke gripped the bowline where it was knotted to the D ring on the front edge of the bow. Tom, behind Gail, reached left and right to grab onto canvas handles glued atop the raft's inflated sides.

"Here we go!" Gail said, as the raft entered the top of the rapid and she altered its trajectory slightly to shoot between a pair of rocks. Roarke howled as the raft snaked over the rapids, the bow rising and dropping, followed by its aft sections as the raft molded itself to the contours of the river like a slinky toy descending steps.

Behind them, Terry back-paddled to slow their entry into the rapids. The angle of descent was sufficient that he only sporadically caught the tops of Gail, Tom, and Roarke's heads as the raft roller-coastered up and down. The sight of Gail sliding into calm water at the bottom of the rough water did little to bolster his confidence. He was scared. Deke had slipped off the seat to ride lower in the raft. "You got this?" he asked Terry, hopefully.

Terry's eyes were huge as he searched for the best course through. And then they were in it. Terry lost control at the pair of rocks Gail had passed safely between. The nose of the raft bumped into one of the rocks, momentarily arresting their movement. A bucket or more of water surged over the partially submerged bow, soaking Deke as the raft compressed itself against the rock, then the stern shot back as the raft recoiled. The current caught the stern and swung it downstream as Terry flailed with the oars, trying to right his course. The oars were alternately catching water and air. The raft continued its descent out of control, bouncing off a rock here, the canyon wall there, finally plunging through the last piece of white water into the pool below.

Gail, who had eased into slack water to watch, pulled hard to intercept Terry's raft like the "pick-up man" in a rodeo who chases down and quiets the bucking bronco, with or without rider.

Roarke grabbed Terry's bowline, and Gail back-paddled for the still water that ran toward the beach from the seam. Soon, the two rafts were slow-gliding side by side.

"Fun, huh?" Gail said, beaming.

Deke and Terry were white as sheets.

"Forgot to tell you one thing," Gail said. "When you see a rock or some other obstacle, and you don't want to slam into it, point your stern away from it and row upstream. The current'll do the rest."

** ** **

Gail loved the ebb and flow of a wilderness river—the very real effect it had on her mind and body. She knew that to surrender to its tempo—*to go with the flow*—was the natural way to be part of the environment. To become one with the rapids and the pools, with the canyon walls and the sandy beaches, with the sun-blasted sections and the dappled shadow of overhanging canopies. Experience had taught her you fight the flow at your own peril. If you embraced it, your body purred with the pleasure of being in sync with nature.

Gail shared those very thoughts with Tom and Roarke as they looked down the barrel of an almost half-mile-long straightaway, gazing at the towering cliff to one side and sandy beach to the other. There were alpine meadows visible on the foothills above the beach. The river was at peace with itself. The rock formations were striking, the striations and different shaded chunks of the canyon wall resembling a giant, muted patchwork quilt. Terry and Deke's raft was visible a hundred yards ahead. Roarke fished from the bow, content to throw his line forty feet out from the raft, mend his line, and watch the big dry fly float without drag . . . its speed matching that of the boat. Maggie sat beside him, studying the water, paying attention when the odd water ouzel skittered away.

Tom had his butt wedged between the stern seat and

the back of the raft, so that his back and shoulders were supported by the juncture to the tubes at the rear of the raft. He tracked a hawk that dive-bombed a nest of sticks seemingly glued to the cliff wall a hundred feet above the water. A pair of concerned parents—swifts in this case— scrambled to intercept him. They under and overed the raptor, nipping at his head and underside, turning their mission into a blur of flying feathers punctuated by a rau- cous squawking at the moments of contact. Sufficiently harassed, the hawk peeled away from the cliffs, deciding to find a meal elsewhere. One of the swifts continued to give him a hard time, escorting him like a sheriff to the edge of town. His partner returned to the nest to comfort their babies. Tom smiled at the outcome of this particular out- door segment. *When Swifts go wild!*, he joked to himself.

Gail back-paddled a few more strokes to put even more distance between their raft and Terry's. Then she shipped the oars, angled her face up to take the direct warmth of the sun. "Tom?"

"Umm?"

"Do Terry and Deke seem funny to you?"

"How do you mean?"

"I don't know, just funny . . . *off*. I mean it's one thing to take an overnight at a campground. It's something else to get on a sixty mile wilderness river and not know the blade of the oar from the handle."

"Ummm . . . you mean just like me?"

"Yeah, but you're with me."

"So are they, thanks to you."

"That's another conversation. I mean, I know some

people are happy going places they've never been. I get that—embrace your inner Marco Polo. But to get on a wilderness river and not know fuck all . . . it just strikes me as being not right."

** ** **

Gail chose a picnic spot she always favored when floating the River Wild. A smooth rock shelf angled gently into the head of a deep, green pool. It was shaded by overhanging pine boughs. She had set up their portable picnic table on the cool stone, just back from where river water dampened the rock. A sandy beach in the sun stretched downstream from the ledge. Both rafts were pulled ashore. The remains of lunch were visible on the table. It was a free period on the river. Maggie and Roarke explored the beach way downstream. Terry was napping in the shaded picnic area. Tom was building a crude architectural model of a house in the sand—using sticks, pebbles, scraps of bark, and so forth. He stood a twig and leaf at one corner of the property—delineated by a line in the sand. It cast a shadow over a corner of the main dwelling. Tom looked up at the sun, then back at his model. He needed more shade at midday. He shifted the location of the twig tree so that the leaf threw more shade over the dwelling. He sat back on his haunches to study the new results. Gail and Deke had waded out into knee-high water on the ledge, where Gail—wearing a one-piece bathing suit—was giving Deke a fly-casting lesson. Deke was shirtless. Gail stepped back to give him some room to cast. Her eyes took in his lean, chiseled torso, his cut arms were sun-bronzed. She might have been less admiring if she knew his fitness was compliments of a daily routine of pumping iron with fellow felons in the outdoor yard of the Montana State prison in Deer Lodge. Nevertheless, Gail was a physical person—physical response was involuntary. Deke's body was better than his casting. She couldn't help but shoot a glance at Tom, on the beach twenty yards away, his slight, unmuscled torso a ghostly shade of white.

Deke tried a cast, but he dipped the rod tip too far behind him and the fly line collapsed in a tangle over his shoulders. "How's that?" he said, grinning.

Gail stepped around in front of him, admiring him from a new angle, trying not to be distracted. "Ah, I think you need some more work. Here . . ." She stepped behind him once more, reached over his shoulder and wrapped her right arm over his. "The most important thing is line control."

"Never had a problem with *them*, before," Deke offered, well aware of her interest, his romantic radar as finely tuned as Gail's hormonal signal.

Gail blushed. She reached under his left arm and took hold of the slack line. Her body touched his here and there. Gail got suddenly nervous, turned on by the contact and the warmth and tautness of Deke's skin. Visibly embarrassed, she started to guide his arms through the motion of casting. "Just remember, ten and two. Ten o'clock on the front end, two o'clock on the back . . . wait a minute for the line to unravel . . . then do it again, ten and two, letting out a little more line with your left hand. So your right hand's your power hand. Your left hand's your control hand."

Tom looked up from his model to see his wife virtually embracing Deke from behind. Tom was not the kind of man to get jealous, so it troubled him when he felt a surge of jealousy surge through his body.

** ** **

By late afternoon they had leapfrogged downriver to another place to pull over and fish. Gail's raft had gone ahead and was beached below a promising riffle that linked the rapids at the head of the pool with the deeper, slower water downstream. Gail sat on her raft, sipping a beer, admiring the towering canyon wall. She had directed Tom and Roarke to start fishing halfway down the pool and work their way up to the riffle.

Upstream, Deke shot Terry a look of concern from his bow position. They were in the tail out of the pool above— twenty yards above the rapids that Gail had recently navigated. The serenity of the deeper, smooth water gave way to the ruckus the interim rapids were making. Terry looked across the top of white-frothed water to the still green pool below. "Fuck me, Deke," he said.

"Just do what she told you."

"Tellin' and doin' are different things," Terry complained, as their raft sped up over the shallow tail-out and plunged into the rapids.

Deke spread his knees on the bottom of the raft for better balance and gripped the canvas straps port and starboard. Just his eyes were visible above the rounded shoulders of the raft. A boulder seemed to race toward them. It cleaved the river, sending tongues of faster water left and right and a rooster tail over the top. Deke turned to Terry and screamed "Boulder!"

Terry flailed at the oars. Everything happened faster in rapids. The uneven texture of the water made it harder to get a purchase with the oar blades. Terry's body kind of jerked this way and that, as a mighty pull on one oar came up empty on one side and dug his oar deeper into the water on the other. He found himself doing the opposite of what Gail had said: trying to push the raft past the obstacle, instead of aiming the bow at it and rowing in the opposite direction.

Deke screamed again at Terry as a collision seemed ever more unavoidable. "She said the other way!! You're pushing us into it!" Deke watched the rock loom larger as if in slow motion. "The other way, *goddamnit!*"

"Hold on!" Terry screamed.

The raft smashed into the rock, catapulting Deke out of his defensive stance and into the froth. His body careened off a few rocks as he flailed his arms and dog paddled to try to keep his head above water.

Gail heard his screams and glanced up just as the current pushed Deke into view, with Terry only yards away, the raft spinning wildly out of control. Deke was swept against another rock and forced underwater. He surfaced a few yards downstream, flailing away, screaming, "Help . . . help!" He disappeared once more as Terry gave up hope of controlling the raft, pulled in the oars, and slipped onto the water-sloshed rubber floor. The raft swung wildly as it was sucked into tongues of current, thrown against rocks, and spun, the bow and stern taking turns leading the way. Finally, it bounced down the final chute and into deeper water.

"He can't swim!" Terry yelled to Gail as the current carried him past her.

Deke, meantime, had also reached deeper water. The final descent had sent him underwater. He righted his positioning by looking up to light and clawed his way to the surface. He swallowed a mouthful of water before catching a breath. He pawed at the water's ever-smoother surface like a dog who hasn't figured out to add his hind legs to the mix. The current pushed him closer to the canyon wall, farther away from the safety of shallow water.

Gail vaulted out of her raft and sprinted downriver in shallow water before diving in at an angle she hoped would intercept Deke. She kicked and pulled hard before lifting her head up to locate him. His head bobbed to the surface. She took a breath and swam with powerful frog kicks and breast strokes toward his body, visible in the pristine, deeper water. She surfaced beside him and grabbed an arm. A frantic Deke tried to crawl on top of her, pushing her under. Their bodies were swept along, entangled, Deke so desperate to get a purchase that Gail was afraid his strength and fear would take them both down. Deke locked an arm over her head, driving breath out of Gail, forcing her to inhale a mouthful of water. Gail knew she was at the brink of passing out. A calm came over her that had surfaced at dozens of dangerous encounters in the past—a reflex born of experience. She let her body go limp, temporarily reducing the force of Deke's grip, then jammed an elbow into his ribs. The blow loosened his grip enough for Gail to squirm out and surface behind him. She gasped for air as she locked an arm across his neck and chest, lifting his face clear of the water. He fought her for a moment.

She yelled, "Stop fighting Deke! You're okay. Just let go. I have you."

Deke puked up water. He coughed and made some growling sounds. He backpedaled with his arms to help steady himself. After a few strokes, Gail could feel the current lessen. She had made it to slack water. She slid from her side to her back and traded her one-arm grip for a two-handed cupping of Deke's head. She began frog kicking for shore. There was blue sky overhead, but the first clouds of the trip started to nudge into view over the rim of the canyon wall.

** ** **

It was coal-black in the canyon. Cloud cover had wiped away even the faintest glitter of stars. The only light came from the embers of a campfire in planned decay. Roarke had turned in—fully marinated by a day of water and sun. Tom and Gail sat on one side of the stone-ringed fire pit, leaning against the rotting trunk of a toppled pine, sipping wine from tin cups. Deke and Terry sat across from them. Silence reigned—a natural state after the close call on the river. Fires stoke contemplation anyway. Add a life-threatening event to the mix, and the meaning of life inevitably rears its head. Deke's face was bruised and scratched. His wet clothes hung from sticks jammed into the ground close by the fire. Terry whittled a stick. A single streak of lightning flared up behind the cloud cover, muted, but noticeable by the sudden pulse of brightness.

"Might get a shower, tonight," Gail said.

Deke peered at Gail's backpack . . . noticed, for the first time in the mesh pocket on the outside of the pack, the handle of her revolver, poking out of its oilskin. He looked at Gail across the fire. She was lost in thought. Deke's face tensed. He shifted his body and ever so slowly slid is hand toward the handgun . . . closer . . . closer. He snatched the .22 from the backpack and trained it vaguely on Gail. "Don't move," he said quietly.

Tom and Gail stiffened, more startled than scared. "What are you doing, Deke?" Tom asked.

"Don't move!"

Terry looked at his partner with visible confusion. "Not now," he whispered.

"Stay still," Deke hissed.

His finger closed on the trigger. Gail stared down the barrel of her own weapon, a bad feeling, compounded by a stupid feeling. Tom braced himself, too paralyzed to react. Deke took careful aim down the short barrel, added a second hand to steady the shot, and seemed to hold the gun for the longest time. . . . *Blam!*

A rattlesnake flew out of the end of the rotting pine log, a foot from Gail's shoulder. The headless snake squirmed for a few feet before ceasing its grotesque death throes.

Tom and Gail took in the spectacle, stunned.

"Must have been sleeping in the log," Deke said. "I can see why you bring one of these along." He turned the revolver around in his hand and offered it back to Gail, grip first. Gail accepted her weapon, still a little shocked. For an old river pro, this was the most scared her family had seen her. "Thanks."

"Got to keep the group leader alive," Deke offered. He pushed himself to his feet, dusted the dirt off his pants. "Anyway, it only makes us even. Time to put this day to bed before anything else bad happens." He laughed. "Though"— he cautioned Tom and Gail with a playful finger—"if bad things happen in threes, we might have one more to go. Night."

Terry stood, dusted himself off, more than anything not wanting to be exposed to questioning all on his own. "Good night, folks."

He and Deke disappeared into their tent, ten yards away.

Gail picked up a stick and reached into the fire pit to scatter the coals.

"This river get any wilder?" Tom asked.

"Oh yeah," Gail reassured him, her normal self-confidence seeping back into her body. She wrapped an arm around his shoulder. "Having fun?"

"Not as much as you and Deke."

Gail withdrew her arm—hurt, and a little disappointed.

"One near drowning. One shooting. One close-quartered casting lesson with a shirtless stranger. Isn't this the perfect family vacation?"

"Tom, don't."

They peered into the fire in awkward silence. "Can we

suspend tit for tat," Gail asked, "at least while we're on the river?"

Tom felt embarrassed and small. He reached out and took Gail's hand by way of apology. "Tell you what. . . . Being on this river's like being inside one of my models rather than looking at one. I'm glad Roarke's seeing it from the inside out. It makes a difference. Makes me see things differently, too."

Gail smiled, pleased. "Good. That's what it's supposed to do."

More silence passed. Their body language warmed. "I think a city kid needs to know what it's about," Gail said. "Just like the country girl needed to learn about the city." She looked at Tom: "And found the right person to help her do that."

"Any regrets?" Tom asked.

"One's good for the heart," Gail said. "One's good for the head. Doesn't mean we have to live in Boston . . . or anywhere else, forever."

She glanced at Tom, hoping to get a rise out of him, happy to have couched her longing in such nonthreatening terms.

"I thought you were the one who told me it snows in some part of Montana twelve months out of the year. Don't you get enough of winter in Boston?"

Gail laughed. "It's a different kind of winter. Urban winter."

"I have to admit there's something purifying about this place, almost as if it reconnects you with something primitive—with your inner animal."

"*Tom Unleashed*. Wouldn't that be a sight to see."

"Watch what you wish for."

Gail squeezed his hand. "Yeah," she exhaled, "back to basics. It's why I like it out here." After a moment: "We used to do better . . . with the basics." Her voice was wistful.

Tom stared at the fire. "We also used to love the differences between us, back when they seemed charming, and hadn't become . . . *just differences*."

The truth filled Gail's face with sadness. The campfire had done it again. Tom knew that poking at their relationship further could only lead to the conversation they had long avoided. He stood, dusted himself off and touched Gail's head. Then he walked back to their tent.

Gail gathered her knees in her arms, rested her chin on top, and stared at the fire. It bathed her face in an orange light. A tear slid down her face. It felt like the end of something.

Later, the fire had died to a few embers, plunging the campsite into almost total blackness. Lightning pulsed again behind the cloud cover . . . closer, brighter. This time thunder followed, filling the canyon with a low rumbling. A breeze ruffled Deke's drying shirt.

Gail crawled out of her tent wearing shorts, a T-shirt, flip-flops and a fisherman's headlamp. She headed into the woods to relieve herself. A stronger gust of wind, soft with the promise of rain, rustled through the camp, lifting Deke's shirt off its branch. A fat raindrop hit a rock encircling the fire pit. Another made a hissing sound as it hit a glowing ember. Gail emerged from darkness to police the area. She lifted Deke's shirt out of the dirt and shook it. A plastic baggie, holding a folded piece of paper, fluttered out of the pocket onto the ground. Gail picked it up and trained her flashlight on it. It was a Montana fishing license. She pressed the baggie flat to better read and twisted her head-lamp to a brighter wattage. The name on the license was *Jim Ladage*. Gail peered at it, confused. She felt physically sick. Her mind went to dark places. She glanced around frantically, to make sure no one was watching.

She twisted off her headlamp so as not to draw attention to herself. Rain started to fall harder, big fat, summer-storm drops, liquid hail that splattered here and there. She retreated in darkness and scrambled into her tent.

She twisted her headlamp back on when she was inside the tent. She aimed it at the tent flap so she could zip it up. She swung the lamp briefly onto Roarke and Maggie, asleep to one side of the tent, the boy's arm cradling the dog's head. She crawled over to Tom, a lump in a sleeping bag on the other side of the tent. "Tom!" she whispered urgently. She jostled his shoulder. "Tom. Wake up!"

Tom rolled onto his back and looked up. His eyes blinked open . . . then blinked some more, blinded by Gail's headlamp. He raised his hand between the lamp and his eyes. Gail twisted the lamp off. "Tom . . . sit up. I have to show you something." She clamped a hand over his mouth. "Don't talk." She removed her hand and twisted her headlamp on again, aiming the beam away from Tom, and into her hands. "Look at this." She held the license closer to Tom's face.

"What? . . . A fishing license."

Gail, frightened: "Look at the name. It's Jim's."

Tom stared at the license. Roarke stirred, drowsily opened his eyes. He had one arm around Maggie.

Tom said, "So?"

"What's going on?" Roarke asked.

Gail nudged his head gently back down. "Nothing, honey. Go back to sleep." Roarke settled back. Gail rubbed his forehead. In moments he was back asleep. Gail swung her gaze to Tom. She was trembling.

"I found it in Deke's shirt."

Tom wrestled to make sense of what she was saying.

"Don't you understand!?" Gail said, leaning closer. "He's wearing Jim's things. And Terry's probably wearing Peter's. No wonder nothing fits."

"Maybe Jim lent him his shirt and forgot his license was in the pocket."

Gail considered that possibility. Her danger radar was on code red. Tom could see her straining to review events. "Tonight," Gail said, "Just before Deke shot the snake . . . did you hear Terry say, 'Not now'?"

Tom gave that some thought. Shook his head. "No."

Gail, on her knees, started to rock back and forth. "Oh shit. Shit, shit, shit. He did say that. I'm sure."

"I don't remember," Tom said. "It's hard to remember anything else when someone's holding a gun on you."

The inside of the tent brightened with a flash of muted lightning. Thunder boomed . . . the loudest yet. A torrent of rain slashed against the tent's protective fly. The sides of the tent pulsed like puffed cheeks.

Deke sat bolt upright in his tent, awakened by the

thunder. He peered at the top of the tent, which was being assaulted by rain. A gust of wind shook the whole tent, then subsided. Deke heard muffled voices—Tom's and Gail's. If the words were hard to understand, the frantic tone was clear. Deke climbed out of his sleeping bag and crawled to the edge of the tent closest to Tom and Gail. Thunder crashed again.

In Tom and Gail's tent, Tom held his wife close to him, doing his best to console her. She felt whiplashed by the day; her emotions spilled over. She was softly sobbing. Rain slashed down onto the campsite. The campfire surrendered with a final hiss and a plume of white smoke. Water began to puddle everywhere and was collected in the pots and pans left by the fire. The whoosh of the rain now overtook the rush of the river as the lead acoustic. Deke was squatting beside Tom and Gail's tent, listening. Water soaked his clothes, dripped from his face. His eyes were fierce, cold, and calculating. Another bolt of lightning—the closest yet—filled the canyon like an outdoor flash, briefly lighting the campsite where Deke squatted motionless, like a maniacal gargoyle. If Tom or Gail had lifted their gaze from one another, they would have glimpsed his ghosty shape momentarily projected on the tent's translucent nylon wall. It was gone in a blink; then darkness. Thunder rumbled close on the tail of the lightning. The full brunt of the storm was getting closer.

12

A solitary truck sent a rooster tail of water into the air as it slogged through the downpour along a Montana highway, hurtling past a rest stop where the lone vehicle was a parked pickup truck with four dog crates. The sixteen-wheeler's red tail lights were still visible when the sound of baying dogs poked through the drumbeat of rain, coming from the dense woods behind the rest stop. The baying grew louder and was soon accompanied by stabs of flashlight beams poking the curtain of darkness. The only other light was provided by an illuminated map of Montana, where a red-circled "You Are Here" reference point indicated proximity to Canada.

The baying grew louder, closer, until a team of bloodhounds burst out of the woods and scrambled up the slight hill to the paved rest stop. Their handlers—one of whom was State Trooper Page Noel—were bundled head to foot in foul weather gear. The dogs pressed their noses to the mud that ringed the paved area, searching for a scent. The mens' boots sunk into the saturated ground. Their slickers shined like fresh enamel paint. Page steered his two dogs over to the map, glanced at where they were and what they had covered. The dogs strained at their leashes, eager to keep going, happy as kids stomping in mud puddles.

The second trooper joined him at the map. "This is goddamn useless, sergeant." The two men peered at the map, seeking inspiration, if not answers.

Page sighed. "If they're out there in this, they're probably drowned, anyway." The two troopers retreated to their pickup truck, dragging their reluctant four-legged partners with them.

** ** **

Trooper Heston stood in the Lieutenant's open door. "Sir, I pulled together those profiles." He handed a file to Long. "From juvenile court records, probation reports, local police records, pre-trial court transcripts, newspaper articles, parole evaluations, informed contact with the suspects. Anything I could find."

"Thank you, Trooper."

Composite Profile

William Deakens Patterson. 38. Born in Big Timber, Montana
Father was a rancher. An alcoholic, he abused his wife and his only son, Deke. State Family Services alerted on numerous occasions. Father beat Deke on

a regular basis. Deke had trouble staying out of trouble in school. One night, Deke killed his father. He was fifteen.

Served three years in Youth Authority Camp. Released on eighteenth birthday under supervised probation. At the age of twenty broke into a gas station and stole a pickup truck out of the service bay and drove it through the roll down door. Was apprehended in Grand Junction, Colorado, extradited back to Montana, and sentenced to six years in state prison. Was a model prisoner, accrued one-for-one good time credits and was released after three years. Six months later police responded to a 911 call reporting domestic violence at a roadside motor lodge. Upon entering the motel room, Deke was found sitting on the bed, shirtless and covered in blood. As he held out his hands to be cuffed, he calmly muttered: "The bitch is in the bathroom, yes I know my Miranda rights and no, I ain't talking. Let's go." Officers found sixteen-year-old Clarissa Woford, a runaway from Great Falls, naked and bleeding profusely from multiple cuts and abrasions to her face and head.

Deke spent six months in the county jail awaiting trial. During pre-trial hearings Deke was attentive and respectful to the judge but oddly confident. As he was led to the lockup after each hearing, he would smirk and wink at Woford. She tried to hide her smile back. Deke faced charges of kidnapping, assault on a minor, and aggravated assault with great bodily injury. A week before the trial, Woford left her mother's house to walk to the 7-Eleven to buy some cigarettes and was never seen again. On the eve of the trial, Deke's defense attorney, Dave Larson, went to see him in jail to let him know the news and to let him know the DA would be unable to proceed and the case would be dismissed. Years later, after retiring, Larson would always remember the look on Deke's face that afternoon in the jail. It gave Larson chills. "He was eerily knowing, as if he already knew the girl was gone." Deke was released from custody.

Diagnosed psychopath. His mother died in a car accident.

Married cocktail waitress Abigail Brennan at the age of twenty-seven. No children. No surviving siblings or parents.

Murdered his wife and his wife's lover two years later when he caught them together in a Livingston, Montana hotel room. Convicted of voluntary manslaughter. Sentenced to fourteen years in a state prison.

** ** **

Composite Profile

Terrance Everton O'Reilly. 35. Born in Manhattan, Montana
Some birth canal trauma led to permanent disability with cognitive processing issues. His parents owned and operated a steak house in Manhattan.

Terry, one of six children, left school after the eighth grade to help in the family restaurant. Terry caught having sexual relations with his younger sister. Was sent to dual diagnostic child sexual abuse treatment facility.

Released in 1995. Had trouble holding steady employment. Worked in the restaurant business at the Big Sky Ski Resort, at restaurants in Billings, Great Falls, and Bozeman.

In 1998 at the Clarry Foundation Group Home for Autism, twenty-year-old Justine Kendrick, an autistic woman, reported to a group counselor that one of the kitchen workers had "stuck his thing in her mouth." Terry was arrested while arriving for the work the next morning and was identified as the suspect in a photo line-up and DNA match. He was sentenced to eleven years in prison for forced oral copulation.

In 2009: Raped two Montana State college girls at a homecoming party at a private residence where he helped cater the meal. Convicted of multiple rapes. Sentenced to twenty-five years at Montana State Correctional Facility in Deer Lodge.

** ** **

Lieutenant Bobby Long set aside the profiles. The wall clock showed two a.m. Rain slanted against the windows of his Great Falls office. A half-empty box of doughnuts was visible on his desk along with two empty bottles of Moose

Drool beer and a half dozen empty Styrofoam coffee cups. Bobby swung his cowboy boots off the desk and lifted himself out of his desk chair. Every part of him was sore. He stretched this way and that. He walked to the window and watched the rain pound down through the light of a parking lot streetlamp.

Trooper Heston walked into the room. "Just heard from Sergeant Noel."

Bobby Long said, "He's wet . . . just a guess."

Trooper Heston shrugged. "That, too. Nothing."

The lieutenant stared out the window. "If there ever was a trail," he said, "there ain't one now. I'd like to think the sons o' bitches are at least shivering their asses off somewhere out there . . . maybe preparing to die of pneumonia." He returned to his desk and offered Billy a doughnut.

"No thank you, sir," Heston said.

Bobby eyed him suspiciously. "Trying to keep your boyish figure, trooper?"

"I'm more of a salt guy than a sugar guy," Billy told him. "Potato chips, fritos . . . "

"One way or the other, we're going to have to put some meat on you."

"Yes sir. That's what my mother says."

"She proud you chose to get into law enforcement?"

"She's happy I'm working."

"Why did you choose law enforcement?"

"My dad's brothers were both cops, in Boston. They told great stories. We had family gatherings on Cape Cod every summer when I was a kid. Jeez, they could talk. And drink. I wasn't sure what I wanted to do, but I liked them, and I liked that they liked what they did. After college, I took the federal law enforcement test and I did okay. I like the traditions of it. I like that there's a right way of doing things, and a wrong way. But I also like that you can follow your intuition, too. Like I see you do sometimes. That you have to think ahead of what the other guys are thinking."

Bobby Long sighed. "How are we doing so far?"

"You'll get them," Trooper Heston assured him.

"It's getting them before they get other folks, that's the assignment. That girl you read about, Clarissa Woford, they never found her. They put her face on milk cartons. Posted reward money. She walked away from her house one night, and Deke walked a few weeks later."

"He was in jail when she disappeared, right?"

"Technically. Physically." Bobby Long looked haunted.

"You think he had something to do with her disappearance?"

"You read the memorandum, his defense attorney thought so."

"And you?"

"He killed her. Or had her killed. My guess is he told her to walk and he'd meet her when he got out. Then he finished what he started in that motel room. She was sixteen. He was an outlaw. You know what they say. Especially small-town girls from broken families. He's evil and smart, that Deke," Bob Long said. "And sick. Stealing. Lying. Killing. It doesn't even register with psychopaths because they have no conscience. It's just a means to an ends."

He walked to the wall map of Montana. His intuition was shooting blanks. The best approach now was good police work. Standard stuff, three yards and a cloud of dust—but always the best way to start. The way pro football coaches would plot out the first twenty plays of a game based on what they knew, and what worked best. Then they mixed it up if that didn't work. Trick plays. Misdirection. When the opponent was William Deakens Patterson, Bobby Long knew it might come down to a Hail Mary. For now, lacking intuition, it was Pawn to E4.

He looked at the big board. Along the Canadian border a dozen tiny plastic police cars were magnetically stuck to the border, representing deployed manpower. He lowered his gaze to an area of the map east of Great Falls, a green, rugged patch called the Lewis and Clark National Forest. There were no assets there, no miniature cars, or helicopters, or tracking dog units . . . only a windy, blue ribbon, romantically named the River Wild.

13

Morning. The storm had blown through, leaving the campsite littered with downed branches and leaves. The river surged with discolored runoff. The camp gear was mostly struck. Gail and Tom secured their gear to their raft at the water's edge. Gail looked drawn. She was red-eyed, fidgety—sleep had been hard to come by. As she lashed a waterproof duffel onto the cargo load, she glanced back at the campsite, where Terry was stuffing his tent into a sack. She repositioned herself on the raft to look downstream without seeming to be *looking* downstream. Deke and Maggie watched Roarke fish. Tom was repacking the food in their cooler.

Gail spoke in a low voice, "How can you even think there might be an innocent explanation?"

"C'mon, Gail, you're the lawyer. Whatever happened to innocent until proven guilty?"

Gail's knuckles turned white as she snugged a knot.

"Look," Tom said, "they're your new best friends . . . not mine. Especially Deke."

Gail glared at him.

"First, they're babes in the woods," Tom said, "now they're butchers. Make up your mind."

"If he touches Roarke, I'll kill him," Gail said.

"Jesus, honey, calm down. I've never seen you like this."

Gail exploded, "Don't tell me to calm down!" Her voice echoed in the canyon.

Terry looked at Gail, visibly curious. Deke glanced upriver, reacting to the tone in Gail's voice.

Gail leaned close to Tom—her voice softer, but knife-edged. "Tell Peter and Jim."

"I hope we get to," Tom said. Then, consoling, "We will."

Downriver, Deke waded up to Roarke's side. He watched Roarke cast and follow the fly intently. He scratched Maggie's head.

"Looks like you're getting pretty good at this," Deke said to the boy.

"Mom says small victories. That's what you get fly fishing . . . a little better each time out."

"It sure looks like fun."

"Real fun, even when the water's off-color, like today."

Deke glanced up at Tom and Gail again. "How would you like to show Terry and me how to do it?" he said to the boy. "Ride with us, this morning."

"I can show you what I know," Roarke told him.

"Well, it's a hell of a lot more than I do," Deke told

him, rubbing his head. "See if you can teach an old dog a new trick."

Upstream, Tom grabbed Gail by the shoulders. "We'll play it safe, okay? As soon as we can, we'll take off on our own. God knows it won't be hard for you to put some distance between the two rafts. Fair enough?"

"I've never been this scared, Tom. Not on this river. Not off this river. That's how much these guys spook me."

Tom kissed her, thumped his chest Tarzan style. "I'll protect you."

Gail forced a smile, then stiffened suddenly, as she heard Terry approach. The big man tossed his tent into their raft, walked off for another load.

Gail glanced downstream at Roarke, bit her lip anxiously. "Roarke, honey!" she yellowed downstream. "Five-minute warning. We're all packed up here."

** ** **

Tom nudged their raft into deeper water. Gail sat at the oars. Terry had wiggled his raft into shallow water and climbed aboard. He sat in the rower's seat, his oars angled into the sand to hold his position. Deke walked up and grabbed the nose of their raft, slid it into slightly deeper water, and saluted Gail. Gail forced a return smile. Roarke reeled in his line and jogged up the beach, accompanied by a barking Maggie. When he reached the rafts, he vaulted aboard Terry's raft with an assist from Deke. Deke quickly shoved the raft into deep water and hopped aboard.

"Mom," Roarke said, grinning, "I'm going to show these turkeys how to fish, okay?"

Gail stood up abruptly in her raft, panicked. "No!" she screamed. Her cry echoed off the canyon wall. The return "Nooooo!" seemed even more anguished. Deke's hard look convinced Gail she had revealed her paranoia. She scrambled to recover her composure, even as Terry dipped his oars into the water and pulled, putting even more distance between the two rafts. "I want you with us, honey, that's all. You shouldn't be bothering Deke and Terry."

"No bother to us, ma'am. I figure he might be able to teach us what the sport's about. When in Rome, right?"

Terry stroked harder for the central tongue of current—roily and nearly chocolate-colored because of the night's rain burst.

Gail trembled as her son moved further away. "Truth is, the fishing won't be any good till the water clears up. Plus, you're not experienced enough on this river to take a little boy."

"C'mon, Mom," Roarke argued, "you always tell me I swim like a fish." Gail looked helplessly at Tom, who was cinching the last duffel. "Tom, you don't think it's safe either, do you?"

"Mom, please. Just till lunch. Then we'll switch back."

Terry straightened their raft in the main current and gave a few strong strokes to start them on their way.

Tom could see it was a done deal. Defusing the desperation seemed the most they could salvage. "I think it'll be okay, honey," he told Gail in a normal tone. "We'll switch in a few hours . . . plus we'll be right behind you all the way."

"Don't worry," Deke said grinning, we'll leave you a few fish."

Their raft gained speed as they locked in with the surging current. Gail offered a brave face, but she was on the brink of throwing up.

** ** **

A few miles downstream, the river entered one of the extended straightaways that punctuated the more frequent succession of back-to-back S turns. Deke and Terry were fifty yards ahead of Gail and Tom, in sight, but out of ear-shot. Roarke cast from the bow of the convicts' raft, happily oblivious to any tension between the boats, let alone the marginal fishing conditions. Tom had relieved Gail on the oars. Gail sat facing him, her butt on the bottom of the raft, her back supported by the bow seat. Maggie stared at the river from her stern position, seemingly mesmerized by the changing bottom and occasional raft-skittered trout.

Tom was doing his best to talk his wife out of her agi-tated state. "You have to admit we don't exactly have the grounds to convict. Right? You're the lawyer, Gail. What's the evidence? . . . Pretty circumstantial. For all we know Jim and Peter could be sitting on the Cape, sipping beers, counting stitches, not bears . . . comparing salt water to their recent misadventures on fresh. Right? It's probably more likely than any of the dark possibilities you've con-jured up. That's number one."

"How could I have been so stupid to let them tag along?"

"Number two," Tom continued, "they don't know we think something's screwy. So that's to our advantage, too."

Gail shook her head slowly. "Then I go and save the guy from drowning. It's so ironic it makes me puke."

"And third, if they are killers, we're in a shitload of trouble, and that's something I don't even want to think about."

Tom cranked the oars a few times, then pulled in his oars so they would just go with the flow.

"Who are they, Tom? What do they want?"

After a long, ominous silence: "I don't know."

Downriver, Roarke was poring over a topo map of the river and the surrounding National Forest with Deke. Roarke had studied this exact map with Gail in their Brookline Village home. "So that's where we camped last night, Bear Flats. And tonight . . . " He traced the curves of the river with a finger. "We'll pull out here, at Sulphur Springs."

"You're really learning your way around these woods," Deke told him.

"Mom always wanted me to," the boy said.

"So where's the takeout?

"A place called Canyon Gorge." He scanned the fold-out map and finally plunked his finger down.

"How far's that from here?" Deke asked.

"Not too far," Roarke told him. "You could figure it out by using the scale down here."

"Rest of the river like this?"

"Mom says there's one scary rapid we've got to run right above takeout . . . right here. And see how close together these squiggly lines get? That means the mountains get really, really steep." His eyes afire, he added, "Mom says the rapids are really kick-ass."

Deke pointed to a narrowing of the river below Canyon Gorge where the topo lines were even more densely packed. "What's below the takeout? Any other places to get off the river?"

"Below Canyon Gorge?" Roarke said, like a boy describing a pirate's treasure map.

"That's the Gauntlet . . . a place you don't want to be. A class of rapids off the charts. Mom told me she ran it once when she was younger . . . and crazy. She said a bunch of people have died over the years trying to run it."

Deke tapped the map below the Gauntlet, "What if you did make it?"

"There's supposed to be an old logging road out. Hardly anybody uses it anymore because nobody's crazy enough to run the Gauntlet."

14

Night and day lost all meaning at Trooper Long's Great Falls State Police Headquarters. The more time that passed without a tip or a lead meant more time for the trail to grow cold. Deke and Terry were not survivalists, so their chances of living off the land long term weren't good. But their prospects of busting into a hunting cabin or lying low in a subsistence ranch at the end of a long dirt road were good. There was a lot of open space in Montana and a lot of antisocial folks who liked it that way. People tended to mind their own business. *Live and let live* was a more common world view than the *if you see something, say something* approach promoted by law enforcement in an era of terrorism. Extended absence from the local community—large or small—would not be seen as out of the ordinary. Bobby Long knew that Deke knew this, and it worried him.

Billy Heston was a millennial, albeit a Montana millennial, if that wasn't a cultural oxymoron. He did know his way around the Internet, which offered a bookend of social media savvy to the lieutenant's old-school "boots on the ground" approach. When he finished the list of things to do the lieutenant gave him, Billy attacked the manhunt in his own way. First, he googled the family histories of Deke and Terry and contacted whatever kin and next of kin he could turn up to see if they had heard from or heard tell of the two fugitives. From the family members willing to discuss friendships either men might have had along the way, Billy widened his circle of possible contact points for the two men. Their mug shots were posted on social media. An anonymous tip line was established. Billy also contacted the family of the long-missing girl, Clarissa Woford, in case the lieutenant's suspicion that she was dead was contradicted by any contact from her, overt or clandestine. Billy warned them that if she were alive, her life was in danger with Deke on the loose. For some, it was the first they heard of the prison break. He also asked for contact information for the girl's friends in case any of them might be in touch with her, or know anything about the man who had courted her and cut her up. His main leverage was that she could be in danger if she were alive and that cooperation with the State Police was the best way to help keep her safe. With that social media web in place, he moved on to a general study of manhunts to see if he might learn something that could aid their own search—an element they might have overlooked or a tactic that could be tailored to the specifics of the Montana manhunt.

When he had finished doing everything he could think of on the computer, he walked into the lieutenant's office to see what else he could do. Long was on the phone, the composite profiles in front of him on his desk, a tuna sandwich off to one side. Billy Heston paced nervously behind him. Long barked into the receiver: "*Find them!* That's what I fucking want you to do!" before hanging up. He wedged half the sandwich into his mouth. "Goddamnit!"

Trooper Heston's face fell. "You did say tuna...right?"

The lieutenant looked at him as if he had two heads. "The *goddamnit* was not for the tuna." He spoke between mouthfuls. "I love tuna. The *goddamnit*'s because we got almost four hundred men, counting the National Guard, shaking the trees of this state . . . and the only thing falling out are pine cones and possums and not the two lifer-psychos who probably couldn't start a fire in the forest if they had a goddamn Duraflame log and a blowtorch. So where the hell are they?"

He grabbed a toothpick and walked over to the wall map. "What if those sons of bitches went south instead of north . . . thinking *we'd* be thinking they'd go north? Misdirection." He tapped the green shaded swath of National Forest surrounding the River Wild. "What if they went here?!"

Trooper Heston looked skeptically at the map. "Nothing in there but snakes and grizzly bears you don't want to know about, sir. They wouldn't stand a chance."

The lieutenant studied the contours of the river and poked at his teeth with the toothpick. "Who? The bears?"

15

Lunch on the river was a test of nerves. The rafts were beached on a patch of sand. The sun beat down hot and hard as it tends to do after a blowout thunderstorm. Roarke and Maggie were prowling the water's edge, looking for crawdads. Deke, Terry, Gail, and Tom sat in the shade of a cottonwood set back from the water, slow-chewing on sandwiches. They considered and vetted scenarios in silence: If we do this . . . they'll do that . . . and if they do that, then we could do this. These thoughts were punctuated by darting eyes, flickered fake smiles that were civil on the surface but excruciatingly tense an inch below.

Terry inspected the remaining half of a roast beef sandwich. "Almost too hot to eat . . . *almost*."

"I could eat in hell," Deke chipped in, "not that I'm planning to visit that particular lunch venue anytime soon. You guys ever eat any of the trout you catch? Or do you always let them go?"

"Most of them we release," Gail said. "I like to keep the

fishery healthy. Plus I don't love the taste of trout. A little bland for me."

Tom lay back, thinking, his head cradled in his hands. Roarke ran up, grabbed an apple and his fly rod.

"I'm gonna see if the trout are hungry, too."

"Where're you going to fish, honey?" Gail asked, concerned.

Roarke shrugged. "Wherever it looks good. Look for heads first . . . everything you taught me. C'mon Mags."

"Fish somewhere in sight, okay?"

Roarke waved a hand as he sprinted off.

"Got a good boy there," Deke said. "Wish I'd learned about the woods when I was a kid. Terry's afraid, but I think I would have liked them."

"I don't like snakes, that's all," Terry said.

"And bears," Deke reminded him.

Terry snorted, "Who the hell likes bears?"

"Where'd you grow up?" Tom asked Deke.

"Oh, here and there."

"What about you, Terry?"

Deke shot his partner a look.

"Same as Deke, really. Here and there."

"Here and there," Tom mused aloud, "population this or that."

Gail curled up on her side next to Tom, providing Terry a glimpse of her white breasts against her tan chest. "That storm kept me up last night. I'm going to take a nap."

Tom settled her head under his arm. "Good plan. My group this way."

Deke stood and dusted off his butt. "Think I'll take a walk."

Terry stayed put, happy to be staring at Gail's cleavage. He slow-chewed his sandwich, imagining he was chewing on her. The thought of doing it for real put a hard-on in his lap and a smile on his face.

** ** **

Deke made his way up the steep slope directly above the lunch site, still visible below. It was one of those river stretches where the sheer canyon had eroded over time, tumbling scree into a wedge abutting the river plain. Spring runoff added silt and soil to the slope, wind and fire planted it with grass and wild flowers. It was a soft, sweet, lush addition to the normal, stone-corseted switchbacks the River Wild was known for. Deke was sweating heavily, puffing hard. He wanted to see what he could see. He liked the protection of the canyons, but it also limited his options.

He walked until the slope gave way to a sheer canyon wall. He looked downriver. He was high enough to see where the straight run they were on gave way to the next set of S turns. But he didn't have the vantage to see where the next takeout might be or, beyond that, where the Gauntlet Roarke described was hedged in by a narrowed canyon. What he saw when he turned his gaze upriver gave him pause. Two fishermen and a guide, in a raft, bounced through the gentle rapids at the head of the straightaway and into the long run. Worry flooded his face. "Fuck." He eyed the zigzag path he had taken to get to the top. He looked downriver, to where the straightaway started bending once more. He half jumped, like a mountain goat, toward the bend. His boots carved divots in the soft soil, but held. He started a controlled jog down the steep slope, leaping and landing in places . . . maintaining his balance, his momentum putting him on the edge of crashing and sliding out of control.

On the river, the fishermen bounced flies off the canyon wall across from Gail and Tom's lunch site. Fishing was slow at midday, the water still off-color. Their guide eyed the beached rafts, the figures in shade. "Want to pull in here and grab a bite?" he asked his clients. "Or keep fishing?"

One of the fishermen glanced over at the rafts. "Let's find a place to ourselves," he told the guide. "No sense of being on the river and sharing it with others. Besides, we might as well float while the fishing's slow and be at a fishier place we can have to ourselves when the sun gets off the water."

Roarke was fishing downstream of the approaching raft, wet wading up to his waist so he could get a fly into the deep water and foam along the cliff face. He stripped in his line and waited patiently for the raft to pass. The guide politely back-oared the raft closer to the shore to pass behind Roarke and not spoil his run. He shipped his oars as he floated close by the boy. "You leaving us any fish, son?" he asked.

Roarke smiled. "A few. Catch anything?"

"Nothing but hogs," the guide told him, leaning over and lifting a stringer with two rubber piggies, one pink, one spotted. Roarke laughed. The guide smiled wide, always happy to get a laugh on the river. He lowered the stringer from sight, extended his oars back through their oarlocks and aimed the raft once more for the main current. "Time to rock and roll," he said to his clients.

** ** **

Terry's face reddened in the noon sun. His snoring overpowered the natural summer buzz of cicadas. Gail's eyes opened. She craned her head to make sure Terry was asleep, then nudged Tom. He sat up immediately, suggesting a premeditated plan was afoot. They crawled away from the shade of the tree and from Terry's slumbering form, afraid a higher profile might awaken him. When they were twenty feet away, Gail popped to her feet and began to jog toward their raft. Tom grabbed her. "Walk! If he wakes up, we're just going for a stroll."

When they reached the rafts, Tom looked around nonchalantly. Terry was still asleep. Roarke was visible, fishing at the end of the straightaway, within sight, as instructed. Gail was frantic to leave. Tom thrust two open palms down, motioning for her to *calm down*. Gail circled over to Deke and Terry's raft and unscrewed the air plug. Then she and Tom each grabbed a side handle of their raft and slid it into shallow water. Tom was watching Terry, not where he was going. His foot caught on a semisubmerged tree stump, and he tumbled over backward, making a sizable splash. Frantic, he and Gail froze. They glanced at Terry, who was still asleep. Gail whispered, "You okay?"

Tom shot her a wobbly hand, mouthing, *More or less.*

Gail slipped over the edge of the raft and climbed into the rower's seat. She carefully extended the oars through the oarlocks. Tom gave the raft a final push and belly-flopped over the gunwale. As the raft glided away, she lowered the oars as quietly as she could into the water. She pulled hard, feathered the oars as delicately as possible so as to not make an unnecessary splash, and leaned into another stroke. Maneuvering the raft in a 180-degree semicircle so she could look directly at Roarke, she positioned the raft in the current on a direct line to intercept him where he fished in waist-deep water.

Maggie, in the meantime, patrolled the inland edge of the beach where the sand gave way to scrub brush. She stopped, stared hard at something, and froze for a moment before lowering herself into a predator's crouch, then bounding off and disappearing into the underbrush.

Just then a trout struck Roarke's fly. Gleeful, the boy shouted upriver to his parents, "Mom, Pop . . . four trout on five casts!"

His voice carried across the water. Gail frantically signaled him to be quiet, but he misinterpreted the gesture. His trout leaped clear of the water. Roarke howled, "Yahoo!" even as Gail shook her head frantically, then drew a finger across her throat. Roarke got the fish on the reel as Gail floated right on top of him.

"Mom, he was right behind the rock where he was supposed to be!"

Gail hissed, "Shush," emphatically pressing a lone

finger to her lips. Desperate, she mouthed, unmistakably: *Shut-up!*

Roarke finally got the message. He looked at his mother and quizzically mouthed, "What's the matter?"

Gail shook her head sternly. Tom extended a hand to Roarke. "Get in!"

"I got a fish on," Roarke complained.

Tom grabbed the leader and snapped it with his hands. "Get in the boat, now!"

Roarke handed his rod to his father as Gail back-oared. Roarke hoisted himself over the gunwale and flopped in the bottom of the raft.

"Where's Maggie?" Tom asked.

Roarke pointed at the brush. "I saw her just before the trout struck. What's going on?"

Tom and Gail both rushed silencing fingers to their lips. Gail glanced frantically at the campsite, then steered the raft closer to shore into slower water. All three peered at the brush, looking for motion and for Maggie's distinctive orange coat.

At the lunch site, a bee landed on Terry's mayonnaise-flavored lips. Terry swatted at the insect, waking himself up. He sat up, looked around; he was alone. He looked toward the river and saw only one raft, half-deflated. His face tensed. He pushed himself to his feet and glimpsed the other raft near the end of the long straightaway, seventy-five yards downstream. Terry started to jog, then broke into a run.

At the raft, Roarke turned to his parents. "Want me to whistle?"

Tom whispered, "No!"

Gail scowled, "Damn it Maggie . . . " Then, "We'll leave her if we have to."

"Somebody tell me what's going on!" Roarke complained. "What's the matter? We can't just leave her."

Tom repeated his wife's sentiment, "We will if we have to."

"We'll tell you everything in a few minutes." Tom stared at the underbrush, growled, "C'mon Maggie, goddamnit . . . c'mon!"

Gail looked downstream. A lone pine jutted out over the water thirty yards ahead.

"If we don't find her by the time we reach that tree, that's it."

Roarke fumed. Tom and Gail exchanged desperate, guilty looks.

Moments later, Terry's voice, echoed in the canyon, "Deke! . . . Deeeeeeke!"

They both turned to see Terry in a full sprint, crashing down the beach toward them, quickly gaining ground.

When the raft passed beneath the angled pine, a covey of mountain quail exploded from the brush at the river's edge. Moments later, Maggie's golden form flew out of the brush and splashed down in shallow water.

"Mags!" Roarke yelled.

The dog began barking and splashed over to the raft, jumped in, and shook her coat. Roarke grabbed Maggie in an affectionate headlock. "Good girl, Mags." He shot his parents an evil eye.

Gail leaned into the oars and pulled hard for the main

current, pulling as if she were back on the Charles, trying to exhaust herself. Tom looked nervously upriver. Terry crashed out of the underbrush and splashed into the shallows at the tail-out of the long straightaway. His chest was heaving. He bent over to catch his breath even as he watched the raft speed up in faster water and bounce out of sight.

Gail expertly navigated the rapids, taking some spray over the bow before steering the raft into the head of the next pool. Deke was standing on a rock ten yards away, holding Gail's .22. The gun was trained on the raft. Gail put her foot on her waterproof bag in the bottom of the raft, hoping to feel her own .22. Nothing. Deke waved them ashore with the gun barrel.

Roarke was baffled: "Why's Deke got the gun? Mom, is that your gun?"

Gail's shoulders slumped. She angled the stern of the raft toward the shore and back-oared.

"Why's Deke pointing the gun at us, Pop? You're not supposed to point guns at people."

The reality of Gail's worst fear coming true filled them with dread. They were dumbstruck. All Tom could manage was, "Not now, Roarke."

When they drew close to shore, Maggie jumped out and started growling at Deke. The fugitive drew a bead on the dog.

"Don't," Roarke yelled, standing up. "You crazy?!"

Roarke flung a life preserver at Deke just as he squeezed off a shot, deflecting his aim. The bullet zipped harmlessly into the river beside Maggie.

Tom bellowed, "Maggie! . . . Get out of here!"

Maggie turned to her master to protest and whimpered.

Deke fired a second shot, missing by inches. He took aim a third time. Tom stood up and threw a coke can at the dog, yelled in a tone that promised discipline, "Maggie . . . go'won!"

Maggie whimpered a final time, and disappeared into the brush.

16

The canyon was as dark as ever that night, but the mood blackened it even more. Terry, holding the .22, sat on a log near the river's edge, watching Tom inflate the second raft with a foot pump. Tom's hands were bound. Gail sat close to the campfire, one arm around Roarke. Deke sat nearby, calmly sipping a beer. The fire crackled and hissed. Tom finished inflating the raft, screwed the cap tight, and was ushered by Terry back to the fire. He sat down beside Gail.

Tom glared at Deke. "What'd you do to Peter and Jim?"

"They're not worrying about you," Deke told him, "so don't be worrying about them."

Roarke looked at his mother, fear in his eyes. "They do something to Peter and Jim, Mom?"

Gail hugged him to her, kissed his head. "I don't know, honey. I hope not."

"What do you want, money?" Tom asked, eager to begin a negotiation that would spark a glimmer of a happy outcome.

Deke retrieved Jim's wallet from his pocket and held up a handful of fifties. "Got plenty of that. Can't spend it out here, anyway." He wiggled free a credit card. "Got credit cards, too." He angled the shiny front of the card in reflected firelight to read: "Jim Robertson. Expires 10-12-20. Not a good thing to be outlived by your credit card."

Tears spilled from Gail's eyes. She cradled Roarke's head in her arms, pressed her head tight to his. She sobbed as she rocked him.

"Course, I don't plan to take until 2020 to get out of here. Which is where you come in." He stood, walked over to Gail and squatted in front of her. He reached into his pocket and pulled out a set of car keys. "We need to get our asses to that takeout, to the rental Jim and Peter had shuttled downriver. Do that for us, and nobody gets hurt."

"You mean, nobody else," Tom said.

Deke removed a switchblade from his boot and flicked it open. He ran the blade gently under Tom's chin.

"*Yeah* . . . nobody else."

Gail's hands were working overtime, practically burying Roarke's head in her lap. Roarke was sobbing now, partly in sympathy with his mother's sorrow, partly because Deke's confession was so inhumanly cavalier. For Gail, helplessness was not a feeling she often encountered, which made it all the more debilitating. Deke left the blade under Tom's chin, then reached over and ran a finger along Gail's cheek. He looked into her eyes. Then he leaned in and kissed her lips. Gail recoiled, disgusted.

"You fuck!" Tom pushed against the blade, drawing his own blood.

Deke stared him in the eyes. "The deal is this: you get us down the river to the takeout, and we all go home."

Tom and Gail exchanged a doubtful look.

"And by my calculation," Deke continued, "that ought to happen sometime day after tomorrow."

"It's at least three days from here," Gail said, "unless you row straight out."

"Fine by me," Deke told her. "I don't mind taking a little more time. Give anybody chasing us a little more time to give up chasing us." He stood and stretched. "It's true what they say about being in the outdoors. Kinda sucks the energy out of you. I'm going to bed. Terry, you got the first watch. Shoot him if he moves. He's no good to us, anyway. Her you got to take care of, least till she gets us past the rapids." He gestured to Tom, Gail, and Roarke. "Thank y'all for an adventurous day on the river." Then he walked to his tent, his swagger reflecting a man in control once more.

** ** **

Roarke couldn't sleep. He was alone in the family tent. He wrestled with what had happened and wondered if there was anything he could do. He groped in the dark for his sneaker and retrieved the knife his father had given him at Hot Springs. He opened the main blade and touched it to his thumb, drawing a bead of blood. He sucked the blood dry and returned the knife to his sneaker. It made him feel empowered.

Tom and Gail were tied into their sleeping bags close by the campfire. Terry sat against a log, his legs snugged in his own sleeping bag, .22 in hand, struggling to stay awake. Behind him a pair of eyes appeared in the dark underbrush. Looking. Moving. Peering. A low rustling sound accompanied each shifting of the eyes. When it was joined by the sound of a stick snapping, Terry's eyes widened. He swung the gun in the direction of the noise. He stared hard into the darkness, trying to make out specific movement. It was all a black, shapeless blur. The rustling sound emerged from another location, yards away. Terry got on his knees and aimed his weapon in the direction of the noise. He was scared. His breathing sped up. When he detected movement and the rustling crackled from another location he swung his gun and fired. The noise filled the darkness with the power of a thunderclap. The next sound was barking . . . followed by a continuous rustling that faded as it feathered into the distance.

The shot awakened Tom and Gail. Tom sat upright with difficulty . . . the crisscross of binding ropes holding him like Gulliver. He heard a final bark. "Go on, Maggie! Get out of here," he shouted into the night.

Roarke's voice floated out of the tent. "Mags okay, Pop?"

"I think so," he shouted at the tent.

Deke emerged from his tent. He looked around suspiciously before walking up to Terry. "The hell's going on?"

"Thought it was a bear," Terry told him.

Maggie whined and whimpered somewhere in the darkness. Deke pinned Terry with a look of disgust. "It's a fucking dog, okay? Jesus. You'd probably shoot your own damn foot if it moved in the dark."

"You know I don't like bears."

Deke leaned closer. "So save the ammunition for *the bears* . . . though a .22's going to piss him off more than hurt him."

Terry looked at the canyon wall across the river, up at the surrounding forest. "I don't like these woods, Deke."

"One more night after this. That's all. Chrissake, don't shoot any trees," he gave Terry a look, "unless they shoot first."

He aimed a finger gun at Terry, mouthed, *Pow.* Then he stalked back to his tent and climbed in.

** ** **

First light angled into the canyon, giving the air a chalky look. The river flowed clear over a gravel bar. A trout rose to take a mayfly, leaving a small, expanding ring on the gray-green surface. Downriver, a raccoon peered into a small pool formed by the log he was perched on. He darted his paw, lost his grip on the log, and fell into the pool. A small trout skittered away into shallow water, rippling the water. The raccoon splashed after it, driving the fish up onto the shore, where it flopped once or twice before the raccoon pinned it with its paws, clamped it in his jaws, and waddled off to have breakfast. High on the granite cliff above the pool, a hawk swooped into a ledge nest carrying a still-struggling ground squirrel in its talons. She settled her wings around her body and looked around for a moment as the rodent tried to squirm free. Then she began tearing the animal apart with her dagger-pointed beak.

17

Lieutenant Long's "ranchette" was not a modern concoction, though the result was similar to what was found in the new subdivisions: a modest, log cabin ranch house with a few small, outer barns set on twenty acres. He had bought the property twenty years earlier from a rich Easterner who loved Montana in the summer and bought a twenty-thousand-acre spread with a trout-rich spring creek for his "little piece of heaven," as he called the property. He had met Bobby back in his rodeo days, at the Last Chance Stampede and Fair at the Lewis and Clark County Fairgrounds in Helena where Bobby won $500 for snagging the Best All-Around-Cowboy award. The Easterner introduced himself to Bobby, then Bobby to his ranch, and sold him twenty acres to be a "ranch manager" when he was around, basically a grandiose title with little responsibility except to train a handful of horses that could be ridden by kids and grandkids. The price was the $500 Bobby had won—a profitable parlay if ever there was one.

Bobby sat on the weathered wood fence, eating breakfast out of a Styrofoam container, watching Marlene, his quarter horse, keep pace with a State Police vehicle making its way slowly down the dirt-and-gravel entrance road.

Trooper Billy Heston parked the car next to the lieutenant and got out. Marlene trotted up, curious, making it a threesome. "Nothing unusual at Hot Springs Campground," Billy said. "I showed the pictures around."

"Guess it'd be a little much to expect them to sign in and reserve a camp site."

Billy rubbed Marlene's head. "How you doin', Marlene?"

"Best damn horse you ever *seen*," Bobby Long said, with as much pride in the rhyme he trotted out with the regularity of a coo-coo clock as in the actual animal. He lifted a forkful of potatoes out of the Styrofoam container. "Twenty-five years that diner's been making home fries, and for twenty-five years they haven't got 'em right. Crunchy . . . goddamn things are supposed to be crunchy on the outside. Soft on the inside, crunchy out." He shook his head sadly. Sighed. "Don't ask me why I keep buying 'em and expect something different. I think it's a variation on the *insanity definition*, home fries division." He offered Marlene a bite. The horse refused. The lieutenant shrugged and shoveled the spuds into his own mouth. "Horse's got more sense than I do. We are creatures of habit, son. All of us. And the more I can figure out that guy Deke's habits, the better I like our chances of catching the son of a bitch."

"Maybe we should send someone down the river," the young trooper suggested.

"And do what? Tell us bears shit in the woods? We need a break's what we need. Something. Let's hope it ain't another body . . ." A look, "Though that might help."

** ** **

The interior of the ranch house was dark and cluttered. White chinking between the log walls kept it relatively draft-free. In the winter, the low stucco ceiling tended to hold the heat generated by a wood-fueled potbelly stove at a uniform temperature, like the lid on a crock pot. A couple of worn Navajo rugs brightened the dark-stained oak floor. A chandelier of deer antlers provided dim light in the living room. One wall bristled with books, stacked on unfinished three-quarter-inch pine planks balanced floor to ceiling on cement blocks positioned at the ends of the eight-foot lengths. The shelves were long enough to hammock in the middle with the weight of all those words. The furniture wasn't much better than what you'd see in a fraternity. There was a dining room table, and a counter with two stools that offered a glimpse into the small, functional kitchen. A hall led to two bedrooms with a bathroom between.

Trooper Heston stopped to scratch Bobby Long's arthritic, twelve-year-old Jack Russell Terrier, Ruby Gallatin. Ruby G., as she was known, came with the last girlfriend to share the home, Paula. Ruby G. stayed when Paula left four years ago, after Bob refused to give her a ring and a commitment, citing something he had read once and believed, that second marriages were the triumph of hope over experience. Bobby's first wife, Mary Ann, died of ovarian cancer seven years into their marriage. Bobby loved her with all his heart; her passing left him with a sadness as deep as marrow.

Paula, who was a little drunk that particular night, explained to the lieutenant that what she was asking for— *after four years*—was nonnegotiable. Which is to say, an ultimatum. The lieutenant thought that over for about ten seconds, cocking his head one way, then another, before walking to the front door and opening it. Paula burned with chagrin, finished her glass of jug wine and flung the glass in his direction. It missed its target and smashed against the wall, leaving a smear of pinot noir on the white chinking. Paula marched toward the door with as much dignity as the situation allowed. "You are such an asshole," she said to the lieutenant. Then she added, in a decided slur, "Keep the fucking dog."

She walked out, climbed into her ten-year-old Toyota pickup truck and drove away into a late-spring snowfall mixed with sleet. The lieutenant was unfazed by the sudden onset of dog ownership. Ruby G., it turns out, had belonged to Paula's son Jason, who had left it with her when he went off to college. He had acquired the dog after a game of beer pong. Bobby Long figured it was a kind of pay-it-forward canine, one whose days were more likely bounded by health than by the prospect of another owner. Truth be told, he was partial to the low-maintenance pooch and particularly liked the fact they both walked kind of funny. A doggie door he sawed out of the front door allowed her to relieve herself as needed. A bowl of water, a stove pot of kibbles, and the odd steak bone were her only demands. On more than one occasion, the lieutenant had confessed to Ruby G. that he wished more women could be like her (though he didn't share that thought with anyone he fancied, being reasonably sure it might be an impediment to romantic aspiration).

Bobby Long, at fifty-nine, had hit a turnout in the highway of life. Except for work, he was happily parked beyond the hustle and bustle of living. He shaved when he felt like it. Left dishes in the sink for days. Liked to put his feet up and drink wine while staring into the coals in his potbelly stove. Women came and went, or didn't. He could have maintained this familiar middle-age, single-male glide pattern for years if it weren't for William Deakens Perkins. Deke reentered his life like a microblast of weather—slamming the front door open, filling the house with a damp, ominous chill. Melodrama was something foreign to the lieutenant, yet in his heart Bobby Long knew he was headed for a showdown with Deke. Man to man. Somewhere. Somehow. The universe called out for it. His certainty in its inevitability calmed him to the events sure to pass before then. It gave him the opposite of anxiety— he believed there would be light at the end of the tunnel.

When the lieutenant left him to change, Trooper Heston stepped up to the cluster of photographs on the dining room wall. He saw his boss in his rodeo days, staying on a bucking bronco, holding a Best-All-Around Cowboy belt. He stared at his first wife, Mary Ann, in full, youthful bloom, a cloud of honey curls, come-hither twinkle in her eyes, blue jeans snug to flesh. He smiled to see the bride and groom on their wedding day, she in a white cowgirl getup and red cowboy boots, Navajo silver bracelets, and a sparkling choker, the lieutenant wearing blue jeans and a brown leather vest over an embroidered white cowboy shirt and bolo tie. The apparent best man stood beside Mary Ann and the maid of honor beside Long, completing the nuptial foursome. Billy stared at the maid of honor for a moment; she looked familiar. The light in the living room was bad, so he lifted the photo off its single nail anchor and held it in the brighter overhead light above the pass-through counter. He stared hard at the bridesmaid and he knew: *Mary Walsh*, twenty years younger, but the spitting image of the woman whose picture lay on his office desk, her neck broken, her lipstick smeared.

18

The rafts were packed and readied at the water's edge. Tom sat in the back of one, with Gail at the oars. Roarke waited patiently onshore. Deke held the .22 while Terry checked the lashings. When he was done, Deke handed him two lengths of rope. "Tie 'em in. Don't want anyone going for any swims without askin'."

Terry tied Gail and Tom by their ankles to the D rings inside the raft. Gail managed a brave face for Roarke, who cowered behind Deke. "Honey, you okay?"

"Why can't I go with you?"

"Everything's going to be okay."

"What about Maggie? She's a city dog."

"A city dog, yes . . . but a dog dog down deep. She'll figure out how to stay alive. I bet she gets picked up by another boat. Just do what they tell you, okay? We're just busing them to the bottom of the river, isn't that right, Deke?"

"That's how I see it."

Tom aimed a finger and a hard eye at Deke. "He's just a boy, Deke."

"Luckily not just any old boy, but *your* boy . . . which makes him special to all of us, if you know what I mean."

Deke grabbed Roarke by the back of his belt and swung him off the ground like a laundry sack. Roarke squealed.

"My group this way," Deke said.

"Pops!" Roarke pleaded.

Tom popped right up in the boat. "Get your goddamn hands off him!"

When he lunged toward Deke, his ankle tether jerked him back . . . making him tumble awkwardly.

Deke released his grasp on Roarke, dropping the boy onto the beach sand. "Okay." He stuck the .22 in the back of his jeans and pulled out his knife. Roarke picked up a handful of sand and threw it at the convict. "Moron!" he shouted.

Deke shielded his eyes with a forearm, then roughly grabbed Roarke by the scruff of his neck and swung him kicking and screaming into his raft.

"Leave him alone!" Gail yelled. Her lips were trembling.

Deke shot Gail a sarcastic look as he marched past her and advanced on Tom with his knife. He flicked the knife inches from Tom's face, "You gotta understand something, Pop. Or is it *Pops* . . . as your boy calls you? There seems to be only one of you, so I'll call you *Pop*, which you should know is actually *one too many* since you're excess baggage on this trip."

Gail struggled against her ropes. Tom stared past the knife blade at Deke's leering face.

"He's thirteen years old."

"So you want me to pick on somebody else?" Deke asked. "How about her?" pointing to Gail.

"You're really sick," Tom told him.

Deke looked away. His knife-free hand lashed through the air and slapped Tom's face with a stinging *whack*.

Deke leaned close, "Feel better, now?"

Tom blinked back tears. "You're something with a knife in your hand and a tied-up opponent."

Gail swung her gaze to Tom. "Tom . . . don't. He's what you said . . . *sick*."

Deke grinned at Gail, mockingly pressed his hand to his forehead as if to take his temperature. He touched the tip of the knife to Tom's chin, forcing him back, back, then struck the blade down, slicing his restraining rope.

He wheeled and flung the knife at a log on the beach, *thwuck*, it stuck in, blade first. "You want a piece of me?"

Tom measured his gusto for an actual fight.

"Put the hurt on him, Pop," Roarke said.

Deke mocked him: "C'mon, *Pop* . . . show the kid what you're made of."

"Don't Tom," Gail said. "He's a killer."

Tom had second thoughts, the logical recalibration of a civilized man. He looked at Roarke, hoping for nonviolent support.

"Guess we know who wears the pants in this family," Deke said mockingly.

Deke shrugged, and turned to get his knife. Tom launched himself out of the boat, his momentum knocking Deke to the ground. They tumbled over and over in the sand, until Deke was able to push him off.

Roarke stood and pumped a fist from his raft. "Kick his ass!"

Terry sat down nonchalantly on the bow of the raft to watch.

Tom and Deke scrambled to their feet and began circling one another—Tom assuming a clumsy, old school boxing stance. Deke stood cockily, his arms to his side, Muhammad Ali–style, turning one way, then the other, feinting a jab with one arm, then the other, shuffling his feet. He was playing with Tom, who ducked back from the purposely short blows. Deke looked at Terry and grinned. Terry shrugged. Then Deke stepped forward and flicked another jab that landed on Tom's face. Tom threw up both hands, as if chasing away a bee. Deke shuffled in and rocked him with a jab from his other hand. Tom stumbled awkwardly. Then he crouched warily, telegraphing his thinking the way nonfighters do. He charged Deke, who sidestepped him easily and drilled Tom with an uppercut to the gut.

Tom sank to his knees and grabbed his stomach, wheezing and gagging. When he rose up, a little woozy, Deke stepped forward and launched another uppercut. This one caught Tom flush under the chin. His head snapped back. His teeth bit his lip. Tom staggered backward, bleeding, struggling to catch his breath. He sank to his knees.

Gail rose up in the raft and tugged on her restraining rope. "No more!"

Tom pushed himself to his feet. One eye was beginning to swell up. Blood trickled from his lip and nose. His breathing was raspy. He faked a lunge, then charged Deke again, head down. This time Deke grabbed his shoulders and drove a knee into Tom's face. The thud was awful. Tom yelled and fell face down in the sand. He lay still for a moment, panting, his hands kind of twitching at his sides.

Gail yanked frantically at her restraining rope, drawing blood of her own. She looked over at Tom, tears in her eyes: "Tom, please . . . be okay," she said softly.

Deke walked over and stood over Tom. "Still want a piece of me?"

"Stay down, Tom!" Gail screamed.

Roarke stared at his father's prostrate figure. Tears filled his eyes. Seeing his father get pummeled was a boy's nightmare. Terry, a few feet away, poked at his teeth, bored. Deke bent closer to Tom, taunting him. He cupped a hand to an ear. "I can't hear you. Still want a piece of me?"

Tom shot out an arm and grabbed Deke's leg.

Roarke erupted, "All right!"

Tom pushed himself onto his knees, pulling Deke's legs out from under him. He crawled on top of Deke and landed a blind punch. Deke jabbed his fingers into Tom's eyes, momentarily blinding him. Deke pulled away from Tom and jumped to his feet as Tom regained his feet. Blood flowed faster from Tom's cuts. He wiped a hand over his eyes, trying to soothe them.

There was a new look in Deke's eye—the twinkle of mischief given way to a killer's stare. The entertainment portion of the program was over. Tom raised his arms to protect himself. Deke stepped in and crashed a right to Tom's face. Tom staggered backward, trying to keep his balance. Deke stepped forward with more devastating blows, a left then a right, each unblocked, each punch piercing Tom's feeble defenses. Tom's bad eye closed entirely. He pulled his fists closer together in front of his face and peered through his remaining good eye. Deke was a blur. The blows landed with gruesome ease. *Whunk. Whunk. Whunk.* With each fist to the face, Tom's head snapped back and his face seemed to swell even more. Deke rested for a moment, shaking his fists out at his sides.

Gail rose up in her raft, pried the oar out of the oarlock and threw it like a spear at Deke. It landed in the sand and stuck for a moment, before keeling over. "Leave him alone!" Gail screamed, her horrifying wail bouncing off the canyon walls and repeating itself.

Tom stood like a drunk, disoriented and defenseless. He staggered one way, then the other, barely regaining his balance with each staggered step, refusing to go down. Deke took a deep breath, shook out his right fist a second time and stepped up to Tom. He peered at him, sadistically turning his head one way, then the other. The final blow came from down under, an uppercut that caught Tom on the chin with a sickening crunch. His head snapped back a final time. His eyes went haywire. His knees quivered and buckled. He crumpled in a heap, unconscious.

Tears flowed down Gail's cheeks. "You fucker-loser-psycho!" she howled. She waited for her own echo to bounce off the canyon walls. She shot out an arm and pointed at Deke. Her next words were more deliberate, her defiant survival mode kicked in. "You touch him again, and I'll never take you down this fucking river. You hear me?! You will never get down this river!"

Deke raised his arms overhead in mock surrender. Roarke's head rose into view above the gunwales—up off the floor of the raft where he had thrown himself to avoid the spectacle his father's final demise. He peered at Tom, blinking through tears. His father lay as still as driftwood, his face mushed into the white sand, discolored in places by blood . "Dad . . . you okay?"

Deke stepped over Tom and marched back to the rafts. "Okay. Let's try this goddamn departure one more time. Sorry for any delay, folks."

19

Viewed from the drop-off and pool below, at water level, the roaring rapids Gail was about to navigate looked like a mogul run on a ski slope. They had to be run in a similar way, a course selected, trouble spots avoided, safety zones identified. Patches of white water and whitecaps were punctuated with deeper, green tongues of water. The acoustic roar was constant. More than on any other stretch, the river's incessant power was felt in its rapids.

Tom and Gail's heads appeared at the top of the rapids, a hundred yards upriver, seeming to hover above the field of white froth. Then they were gone, swallowed into a trough, only to shoot up once more, preceded by the black nose of the Avon raft. Tom, at Gail's direction, had sunk down into the bottom of the raft. He clutched the canvas handles to either side. His face looked like a puffy platter of hamburger. One eye was swollen shut, underlain by a black-and-blue shiner. Dried blood stuck to his lower lip. Gail manned the oars with strength and precision, riding the rower's seat like a rider on a bucking bronco, using the oars for balance and guidance, making a continual series of small course corrections to pick the safest route through. Her raft did one more trough plunge and upward thrust before bumping into the quiet pool below.

Safely through, she back-oared for the beach side of the run, away from the canyon wall. She steered the raft into a back eddy, which held it in a constant, slow-moving holding pattern. "I'm going to hold here, honey, in case they get in trouble. We'll be in a better position to help Roarke."

Tom lifted himself off the raft's floor and onto the stern seat. He was drenched. He shivered in the shade. "You're really good at this," he mumbled to Gail. His speech was a little bruised.

Gail smiled. She was embarrassed by the compliment. "It's only rowing."

"Somewhere along the way I stopped admiring you for what you do well, and started competing with you." He reached over and brushed her damp hair. "I'm really sorry about that."

"Not always right, but never in doubt," she mimicked. "I can be pretty bossy." She took Tom's hand in hers. "You don't look too good." Gail peeled off her t-shirt, dunked it in the river and wrung it out. She pressed it gently to Tom's face.

Tom started to laugh, but it hurt too much. "I was doing my best rope-a-dope . . . 'cept I think I was the dope for letting him goad me into fighting." Tom brightened. "Think I hurt his hands?"

Gail smiled lovingly, "You killed his hands. I know

that for a fact." She couldn't stop a giggle. She clamped a hand to her mouth, but it was too late.

Tom giggled back, involuntarily. "Ow . . . "

Gail touched his hair. "Sorry."

They looked into each other's eyes for the longest time. Gail's thoughts went to a darker place. "They're going to kill us before we get to the takeout."

"They'd like to," Tom said.

"Tonight's the last night. We need to do something while they still need me."

"Like what?"

"If it really gets down to it . . . I'd rather dump us and take our chances in the water."

The specter of a kamikaze mission sent them into a quiet funk.

"Where? Indian Rapids?" Tom asked.

Gail nodded. "I know just the rock."

"What about Roarke? We made him together."

Gail fought off tears. "I know," she sobbed. "And it makes me so . . . mad . . . but I don't know what else to do."

Tom engulfed her in a hug. "You know we're going to get out of this, right? You know that," Tom said.

"I like your *never in doubt*, part," Gail replied.

"Except *right*, too!" Tom told her.

"Yeah," Gail said, softly. She savored the incongruity of confidence rising Phoenix-like out of a face that belonged in an emergency room. For the first time in a long time, Gail surrendered to Tom's strength. She hugged him with all her might and tried to believe him. "I can't believe Jim and Peter are dead," she said. "Their families don't know, Tom. Right now, they don't know. They're doing whatever they're doing, and *they don't know.*" She started sobbing again. "They think they're safe *with me.*"

"You can't look at it that way. You know what I always told you: when your time's up, there's no negotiating. That's what happened, Gail. You weren't even on the river." A sadness overcame Tom. His own survival and the well-being of his family had preoccupied his thoughts. He blinked away tears. "They were so happy to go on this fishing trip."

"I know," Gail said, "that was the last time we saw them alive . . . at our home, the night we fought. If you had talked me into not going, they wouldn't have gone either. They'd be disappointed, but alive."

Tom found strength from somewhere. "We owe it to them to get out alive, Gail. To make sure their killers never kill again. To put them away for good. It's not just our lives we're saving, but others. We owe that to Jim and Peter. Okay?"

"Okay," Gail said softly.

** ** **

Terry's terrified yelp punctured their relative quiet. He was at the oars, but he wasn't in control. They were staring at the final stretch of the rapids, and the raft was broadside to the current. Deke hung on behind Terry, eyes wide. Roarke was on his knees in the bow, holding onto the bowline where it was knotted to the bow D ring. His eyes peered over the front of the raft; his face was ashen. He saw a boulder rushing at them. He threw himself to the upriver side of the raft to unweight the downriver side and facilitate the raft's ability to roll over the rock. It slid up and over and splashed down.

Deke got knocked sideways in the stern. He re-secured the .22 in the back of his jeans and fumbled for the canvas straps. Terry managed to maneuver the bow downriver in time to face the last obstacle: a trough and ledge. "Aw, fuck . . . hold on," he yelled. He pulled on the oars but got only air because he was angled too far backward. The bow of the raft dipped suddenly; they seemed to be falling into a hole in the river. Seen from below, Roarke's head bounced into sight first, then Terry's, then Deke's as the raft snaked its way over the ledge and shot straight up. Terry tried to steady the landing, but his oars hit the water at different times, to different depths, jerking it sideways once more. They careened off a rock and were slammed against the side of the cliff. The force of the current held them against the cliff wall, on a straight course, banging, banging, banging the granite. Terry tried to ship the oar so it wouldn't keep hand-braking against the cliff, but the power of the current sucked it out of his hand, and he tumbled backward. There was one final plunge, then the raft shot through a wall of spray and landed into the safety of quiet water.

Gail had begun moving downriver when she saw them in the last section of the rapids. It only took her a few strokes to angle downstream and into the main current. She expertly stoked her raft alongside Deke and Terry. Roarke grabbed the canvas bow strap on Gail's raft. Gail back-oared the two rafts out of the faster current and into the slack water opposite the cliff. She beached both rafts at the tail end of the pool. The gear was removed, the rafts were tipped on edge to drain the river water.

Deke looked a little nervous. "How does that compare to the final rapids?"

"It doesn't." Gail said, walking away.

"Guess who's driving?" Deke shouted after her.

Fifty yards above them—at the tail end of the rapids—a green canoe expertly navigated the last ledge and chute, and shot into the deep water start of the run. The rower's khaki-and-green uniform indicated that he was a Fish and Game ranger. Deke ran up and corralled Tom and Gail. "Not one fuckin' word," he told them. He brandished the .22 for them to see. "Terry," he barked, "get the kid."

Terry clamped an arm around Roarke's neck and pulled him slightly apart from the group. He clicked open his knife with his other hand for Tom and Gail to see. Then he cupped the blade.

The ranger beached his canoe and hopped out. He was in his late twenties, sinewy, dark skinned, part Indian. "Afternoon, folks."

"Howdy," Tom said.

The ranger wiped his face with a bandana and stuffed it back in his pocket. He gestured behind him. "That chute's trickier than it looks, even when you've been down it a dozen times. How's the fishing?"

Gail held her silence until Deke gave her a look. "Catching a few."

"Glad to hear it," the ranger said. "Water only cleared

up last week. Hell of a snowpack this winter. Runoff hit seven thousand CFS two months ago."

The ranger sensed an awkwardness. Folks on the river—particularly after some long stretches of solitude—tended to enjoy a little "country store" chitchat. He looked from face to face, took in the unusual positioning of bodies and the stiff postures. His gaze settled on Tom's face. "What happened to you?"

"Got tossed out of the boat in one of the rapids. I moved, the rocks didn't."

"Done that myself a time or two."

Gail was practically bursting. She looked at Deke, then Terry, and smiled at Roarke. Tom eyed Deke's gun that was tucked in his belt. He spotted Terry tightening his grip on Roarke. He debated his options. He lifted one toe ever so slowly and began to carve an SOS in the sand.

"The river doesn't get any easier below here," the ranger said. "You folks have the proper life jackets for everyone?"

"We're covered," Gail said. She stepped forward and put out her hand. "I'm Gail MacDonald . . . used to be Gail Anderson before your time. I must have guided this river fifty times about a million years ago."

They shook. "Nice to meet you, Gail," the ranger said.

"That's my husband, Tom, and son Roarke over there. I could run Indian Gorge in my sleep, but thanks for the heads-up. Most folks that float the river for the first time tend to underestimate it."

The ranger ran both hands through his hair, then glanced up at the sun. "Been on the river for a week. I better get going if I'm going to get off by nightfall. Have a safe rest of your trip." He started for his canoe.

Tom blurted, "Officer!"

The ranger stopped. Terry hoisted Roarke against him so that only the tips of the boy's sneakers touched the ground. Deke swung a hand around and gripped the pistol handle.

Tom's eyes shined hopelessly from his poor-excuse-for-a-face. "I was wondering . . ."

He deliberately stared down at the SOS he had carved in the sand—trying to direct the ranger's attention. Tom's gaze settled on a trout fly stuck to his fishing vest. He plucked the fly from the sheepskin patch, improvised, ". . . if you knew what the hell this is? Seems to me the only fly the fish are interested in. It's my last one."

"Let's take a look," the ranger said, marching over.

Tom looked down again at his SOS, praying to himself, *Dear Lord . . . give this ranger the wherewithal to look down . . .*

"Looks like some sort of caddis," the ranger said, examining the fly.

Tom desperately tried to position the ranger to look down. It was a silent, awkward tango. Deke stepped beside Tom. His boots covered the SOS , and with a slight shuffle the message was gone. Tom glanced down and saw Deke's sabotage. Deke clapped him on the shoulder, feigning interest in the fly discussion, mocking Tom with the gesture and a subsequent grin.

"Might try a humpe or a stimulator," the ranger told

Tom. "These aren't the finickiest trout in the world, but they are trout. Whatever works, works. As a fishing guide explained it to me: 'No matter what anybody tells you about where to fish, or when to fish, or what to fish with, the singular truth about fishing is you won't catch anything if your bait's not on the water.' Tight lines."

He retreated to his canoe, slid it into the river, pushed off, and jumped in. Gail viewed him like a shipwrecked refugee watching a ship passing by her deserted island. Her face fell. Something snapped. Her feet started to move. "Come back," she said softly. Her walk turned into a trot. The ranger was still in view, paddling hard in a swift current to push himself ever faster downriver.

"Gail?" Tom said.

Deke glared at Tom. "Where's she going?"

Gail was running faster and faster, driven by a mother's desperation.

"Get her," Deke yelled at Tom, "or the boy's dead!"

Gail stopped running to scream: "Come back!"

Tom took off after her. Terry, downriver, pushed Roarke to the ground and started at an angle to cut off Gail. Deke also gave chase.

In his canoe, the ranger paused to slide his headphones over his ears. "Route 66" filled his head, proper fuel for the last stages of a journey. Gail watched the ranger steer his canoe into the tailwater of the pool.

"Stop her!" Deke yelled.

"Come back!" Gail yelled, hoarsely.

"Get her, Terry!" Deke shouted.

Gail splashed into the shallows, then onto a rock shelf below which the river dropped into a cauldron of churning water.

Terry bounded after her, closing in. As he reached to grab her, Gail dove into the pool. Tom and Deke rushed up beside Terry. The three men peered into the deep, churning water that looked like green Guinness. The water moved in a kind of vertical eddy, rising up close to their feet at the edge of the ledge, surging upward against the rock face.

Tom swept his eyes downriver, looking here and there "Gail!" he called out, but his voice was swallowed up by the roar of the river.

"Where is she?" Deke asked, anxious. He pointed an angry finger at Tom. "You gotta find her."

On the beach, Roarke was chugging toward the three men as fast as his legs would carry him. He was huffing and puffing with the exertion. Tears squirted out of his eyes. "Mom!" he wailed. "Mom!"

Tom looked downstream from the ledge. No sign of Gail. His bruised face began to shatter. "Gail!?. . . *Gail?!*"

Deke was livid. "Come back, goddamn it. Come back!" Then he screamed like a kid having a tantrum, "We need you, you hear me? We need you!"

Tom started to lose it. "Gail?" he warbled, weakly. Nothing. He threw himself into the pool. Beneath the surface, all he could see was the white churn of bubbles wirled by currents. It was like being suspended in the middle of a blizzard. Above him, on the rock ledge, Deke and Terry stared anxiously here and there. Losing your driver on the River Wild was not a good thing. Losing control stung even more. Tom's head popped up. He treaded water for ten or fifteen seconds, sucking in air. Then he took a deep breath and dived under once more.

Roarke joined Deke and Terry on the edge of the ledge where the water was only a foot deep. When Tom's head popped up again, he screamed, "Find her, Dad. Find Mom!" His face was tear-streaked.

No one saw Gail's head rise up ten yards behind them from a pothole the size of a manhole cover carved by hydraulics into the ledge. The water was a little deeper there, maybe two feet. Gail gasped for air in silent sucks. The soundtrack of the river covered up those breaths, as well as the slight splashing as she rose up through the pothole and crouched at its edge. She eyed the men and Roarke. She spied the handle of her .22 poking out of the back of Deke's belt. She eased her way downstream in a half crouch. Deke and Terry were staring into the pool as if mesmerized. Gail eased up behind Deke and snatched the weapon. Deke whirled around, startled. Gail aimed the .22 at him and backed up a few steps to get more clearance.

Roarke's face exploded happily: "Mom!" He scrambled toward her before Deke thought to grab him.

Tom's head appeared once more behind Deke and Terry. He saw Gail holding the gun, with Roarke beside her. His smashed-in face brightened. He breast-stroked downstream and climbed onto the ledge far away from the fugitives. He gave them a wide berth as he made his way to Gail and Roarke.

"How'd you do that?" Deke asked, baffled. "God-damn, you do know this river."

"Tom, get Roarke and get in the raft."

Deke and Terry started to edge apart.

"Don't move, or I'll shoot," she warned them. Her words were firm, but her eyes darted and danced nervously. Her gun hand quivered.

"I doubt it," Deke said. He stepped toward her. Gail clamped a second hand on the grip and drew a bead on Deke's forehead. She started to back up toward shore and the rafts. "Hurry, Tom!" she shouted.

Tom hoisted Roarke into the front of the raft.

"Now take the hatchet and slash the other raft!"

"You don't want to do that," Deke said, shaking his head.

"Sink it, Tom!"

"Darlin', you're doin' the wrong thing. I'm telling you the truth."

"Shut up! Do it, honey."

Tom grabbed the camp hatchet and slashed away. The Avon collapsed into a heap of rubber.

Gail glanced over her shoulder at Tom and Roarke. "Row into shallow water."

Deke shook his head and stepped closer toward Gail. Then he reached into his pocket and held up a fist. He turned the fist palm up and opened his fingers slowly. Six .22 bullets were visible.

Gail's face fell for moment, then, "Nice try. You can keep all the extras you want. They're no use without a gun."

"I may not be the hottest thing on the river," Deke said, "but long ago I figured out that running rapids with a loaded pistol in your pocket was a shortcut to the soprano section."

Tom and Gail exchanged anxious looks. "He's lying," Tom said. "He's good at it."

"I'm going to take that as a compliment, Tom. I'm also going to give Gail to three to show me what kind of attitude she's got. One . . ." He took a step toward Gail. "Two . . . " He took a second step.

"I swear I'll pull the trigger, Deke! You know I will."

"Make it easy on all of us . . . *three.*"

Deke stepped even closer, taunting her. Gail's finger squeezed the trigger. *CLICK.* A terrible click. Panicked, she squeezed again. *CLICK. CLICK.* Deke's hand closed over Gail's. He bent her wrist back and forced her to the ground.

"Go Tom! Take Roarke . . . go!"

Tom dipped his oars in and pulled for deeper water. He felt a horrible dread in his stomach. The situation at hand was too overwhelming to consider in a logical way: *Row away and save Roarke. They need Gail to get down the river so they won't kill her. I can get out and get help before they can get off the river. Maybe . . .*

Deke dragged Gail by the wrist closer to the water's edge. "Look at her, Tom! You're looking at her for the last time if you do what she says. And that's the truth, too. Just like the bullets."

"Save yourselves!" Gail yelled defiantly. "I love you, Roarke! Go!"

Tom looked back and forth between Roarke and Gail. The boy shook his head. Tom's swollen face trembled with indecision. The current tugged his raft slowly downstream. Roarke abruptly threw himself out of the raft and began swimming to his mother.

Gail's body sagged. She shook her head. "No, honey. Go back. Go back with Dad. Get downriver!"

"I'm not leaving you the way we left Maggie."

Tom's shoulders sagged. He dipped his oars in the water and took the first stroke toward shore.

Gail wailed, "Noooooo!"

Deke released his grip. She slumped into a fetal heap on the beach, her body wracked with sobs.

20

Terry held a bottle of Jim and Peter's whisky in one hand and an armload of tinder and wood under his arm. He stepped across the fire pit, dumping the wood like a water drop from a firefighting plane. The wood, a mix of dry pine cones, dead limbs, and needles settled into the embers. Combustion took only a matter of seconds. The dry fuel and pine tar crackled and flamed up, sending sparks into the air. "Last night," Terry said, already drunk. "Calls for a little celebration." He took a seat on a log. "Maybe we should have an awards banquet. They do that on these kinds of river trips don't they?"

Deke ignored him. He sat nearby, studying a topo map of the river, chewing on a hot dog, sipping a beer. Tom and Gail sat across the fire from Terry, hands bound behind their backs, Roarke between them.

Gail glared at Terry. "Why'd you have to come to this river? . . . To this beautiful place? Why?"

Terry only smiled. Deke took a last chomp on his

hot dog. "Our first choice was Canada," he told Gail. "But then we figured *they'd* figure we'd make that move. So we made 'em think it was. *Him* more than them, probably. There's one trooper who's not going to be too happy." The prospect of Lieutenant Bobby Long busting a gut put a momentary smile on Deke's face. He took a long pull on his beer. "Hated to give up the car, but they were probably onto that, anyway . . . so we ended up here."

"But now I'm wondering, after looking at this map, if *Montana's finest* might be figuring *if we did* get on the river, where would be the first place we could get off?" He held the map in front of Gail and pointed at the takeout. "Which is right here, according to Roarke. The good news is there's a car there we have the keys to and can find once we aim the clicker at the parking lot and see who blinks back. A car that's supposed to be there and driven away. The *bad news*—and like you, Gail, I always like to know what the bad news might be—is that there might also be a welcoming committee, providing *someone* was smart enough to figure out what we did, especially after coming up empty-handed at the border. It'd kinda be a *prime lie* for law enforcement, you know. I now know what a *prime lie* is because I heard you tell Roarke it's that place on the stream where a confluence of food, oxygen, and shelter makes it the place where the biggest fish hang out. If I were a big fish with a badge and a gun, and this was the first and best place to gobble up whatever was coming down the river, wouldn't I be there? Especially if the big fish was carrying a grudge, for some reason. Not to mention that ranger we saw. What if *he* started thinking about how stiff our little group was, how beaten up Tom's face was, and what if he did see Tom's SOS before I could step on it but didn't say anything because he knew we only had one place to get off and reinforcements might be a good idea. You know what I'm saying?" Deke tapped the stretch of the river below the takeout. "Roarke called this the Gauntlet. Said it was what made the River Wild really wild. What if we bypassed the main takeout, to be safe, and went down here to this logging road at the bottom?"

"You can't do it," Gail said.

"I know I can't," Deke said. "But you can."

"It's suicide. Do you know how they describe class VI? Nearly impossible. Any attempt will result in injury, near drowning, or *death*."

"But Roarke told me you ran it once."

"Yeah, a million years ago. When I was a little crazier, and I didn't have a family to worry about."

"Exactly my point," Deke said, carefully refolding the map. "Now you *do* have a family to worry about." He tapped his temple with a finger, then backed off.

Terry took a sip of whisky and handed the bottle to Deke as he walked by. His ingrained anxiety about the wilderness—and all its creatures lurking within—had given way to the power of drink and the expectation that the end was in sight. It made him happy. Gregarious. Horny. He walked over to Gail and knelt beside her. "And tomorrow, after you get us through those rapids . . . or those rapids below those rapids . . . " He stroked her cheek. Gail recoiled. "Just you, darlin' . . . and *me*."

Tom lunged at him. Terry, even drunk, was ready. He

smashed his forehead into Tom's head, sending Tom slumping backward like a crash dummy. Terry peered at Tom. "You sure got a big appetite for getting beat." Then he stood, looked at Gail once more. "Better rest up." He staggered off.

"Sorry, Mom," Roarke said softly. "He was asking about the river before all of this happened."

Gail smiled at him. "I'm glad you know the river, honey—want you to know the river. That's a good thing." She glared at the retreating Deke. "Deke!" she shouted. Deke stopped but didn't turn to face her. Gail's eyes burned with hate. "You better know something about the woods." Deke hoisted the whisky to his lips and drank. Gail's voice trembled, "You better know there's an order out here . . . a balance. Everything has its place. The rocks, the river, the fish. The trout eats the mayfly and the hawk eats the trout. But *nothing* kills for nothing. It's been going on this way forever and ever." Silence. The fire crackled. The river whooshed. Gail spoke with a new resonance; to her, this was religion. "Somehow. Somewhere. Sure as rain. If you break that order, *you will be broken!*"

Deke casually removed the .22 from his waistband and placed the barrel to his head to mock Gail's prediction. "Might as well just get it over with then," he said to the sky. He walked back and squatted in front of Gail. "Maybe, you're right," he told her, "but there's a lot of laws. And I've spent a lifetime breaking most of them." He calmly touched the barrel of the .22 to Gail's forehead. "But the one I like the best, the one I believe in the most, is the law of relativity. And right now, *relative* to you, I kind of like my position." He mouthed, *Pow*. He smiled and returned the gun to his waistband. "Midget—in the tent!"

Roarke wrapped his arms around Gail's neck. "I love you, Mom."

"I love you, too," Gail said.

Roarke wrapped his arms around his father. "Everything's going to be okay, Pop."

Unseen by Deke, his hand searched out Tom's, transferred his palmed gift knife to his father's hand, then closed his father's fingers over it.

Tom squeezed his fingers tightly around the knife. He hugged Roarke. "I love you. You make me so proud."

Roarke looked at Tom's beaten face. "And you always make me proud," the boy said. "Love you, too."

"Okay. Everybody loves everybody," Deke said, impatiently. "Terry and I love you all, too. It's a big love fest on the river. You walkin' to your tent, little big man . . . or do you want a ride."

Roarke popped up and walked past Deke, giving him a wide berth. Deke handed Terry the .22. "Okay campers, lights out. Big day tomorrow."

Tom and Gail struggled to their feet; their bound wrists made it difficult to stand. Deke took Gail by the elbow and led her to the tent. He waited for Tom to climb in with her and wiggle into their sleeping bags. Then he zipped up their sleeping bags, and then Roarke's, and lashed each bag with a length of rope. "If you gotta pee, call the guard and get a hall pass. Sweet dreams." He backed out of the tent and zipped up the front flap. He walked past Terry en route to their tent. "We'll shorten the shifts to two hours. You take the first. Wake me for the next."

Terry threw more wood on the fire, then dragged his own sleeping bag to the base of a nearby pine tree. He wiggled his legs into the bag, got comfortable with the pine trunk as a back rest, and took a sip of whiskey.

** ** **

A few hours later, a breeze stirred in the canyon as a near-full moon peeked over the cliff across the river from the campsite. It angled its brittle, blue-gray light onto the river through the pine boughs, giving them new definition, and onto the colorful tents, brightening them like Chinese lanterns. The fire had been reduced to a bed of coals. A sudden gust made them burn fiercer, hiss softly. Pine boughs danced overhead. Terry snuggled deeper into his sleeping bag, its warmth, combined with the inner glow of whisky, conspiring to put him to sleep.

In Tom and Gail's tent, moonlight filtered into the dark space as if it were on a rheostat, filling the space with a warm glow. It reflected off the tip of the knife blade Tom poked though his sleeping bag. He sawed the blade up and down, working his way through the restraining ropes. The blade looked like a shark fin moving across the bright-blue shell of his sleeping bag. Tom patiently sawed through the remaining rope and sat up. He unzipped his bag with his now-free hands. He heard Gail's soft breathing, and peered at her face visible in the oval head hole of the mummy bag: it was lined with fatigue and given over to sleep. Roarke, too, was asleep.

Tom crawled out of his bag, gently touched Gail's and Roarke's heads—almost like a blessing—and slowly unzipped the front flap to minimize noise. He slipped out of the tent, zipping the flap behind him. On his knees, he glanced at Deke's tent: all was quiet. He looked for Terry, didn't see him, then crawled to the far side of his tent for a different vantage. Terry was asleep beneath a towering lodgepole pine. The full moon emerged from behind fast moving clouds. Tom flattened himself to the ground. Moonlight brightened the campsite like a prison beacon. Tom waited. When a new thicket of clouds raced toward the moon, he pushed himself onto all fours. He started toward Terry, gripping the knife in his right hand. Hand forward. Knee forward. Stop. Listen. Other hand. Other knee. Stop. Listen. Terry sputtered in his sleep. Tom dropped once more to the pine needles.

The upstream wind grew stronger, softly rustling the boughs of saplings and towering pines alike. Tom looked up. From his angle, the shimmering, feathery lodgepole limbs wiped the black sky momentarily free of stars. They reappeared when the gust subsided. Tom waited until Terry's breathing evened out again, then he rose up once more onto all fours. He gauged the distance to his prey: only a

few more yards. He took a deep breath and inched ahead.
Hand. Knee. Stop. Other hand. Other knee. Stop. Terry's
boots loomed in front of him. Tom lowered his torso to the
ground and crawled to one side of the inmate, to get in a
better striking position. Satisfied, he pushed himself to his
knees once more. Then he eased onto his haunches. Terry's sunburned face was angled away from him. He lay on
his back, offering a big target. His right hand held the .22.
Tom swallowed hard and raised his knife hand overhead.
Being a moral man, the thought of what he was about to
do—kill another man—gave him sickening pause. He lowered the knife and wondered, *Is there any other way to save
my family? Maybe just knock him out with a rock.* . . . He
looked around and saw only a smooth carpet of pine needles. Time was of the essence. Back to Plan A. It was self-
defense and would surely be viewed as such in any court of
law. But nature's law was what consumed him now. Was
he violating Gail's dictum that nothing killed for nothing?
But this wasn't nothing. This was survival. A taste of blood
from his puffed and cracked lip reminded him. He raised
his knife.

The fugitive's eyes popped open. He blinked once,
twice, then suddenly sensed Tom's presence. Tom drove
his knife hand down just as Terry reflexively rolled away,
throwing up his left forearm instinctively. More than one
prison attack had honed his survival instincts. His arm
deflected the blow, but the blade drew blood. Terry tried
to retaliate by lashing back with his other hand—the one
holding the gun—but the gun went flying as he swung
wildly at his assailant.

Tom drove the knife a second time, but the convict tumbled away from the blow. He struggled to kick himself free of the sleeping bag. Tom pounced a third time, hoping to press his advantage. Terry grabbed both of Tom's wrists and threw him back with ease. He grabbed the flaps of his sleeping bag in both hands and yanked them apart. The bag split in half. Terry scrambled to his feet as Tom got to his and advanced on the inmate in a crouch. Terry swept up the sleeping bag and wrapped it around his forearm as a shield. He angled that forearm toward Tom. The men circled one another. Tom held his knife warily, the advantage of surprise now gone. Terry enjoyed his visible discomfort. "You are a glutton for punishment."

Tom lunged with the knife. Terry deflected it with his padded forearm and the blade sliced the fabric, loosing down feathers but doing no damage. Tom's eyes darted to the ground, searching for the 22. He spied it, but Terry read his intentions and sidestepped to put himself between Tom and the gun. Terry began to step toward the weapon, eyeing Tom all the way, daring him to attack. Tom made one lunge, but Terry swatted it away with the forearm and hit Tom with his other hand. Tom staggered backward. His chances of beating Terry to the gun were nil. He bolted.

He ran past Deke's tent and plunged into the semi-darkness of brush. The moon burst free of clouds once more, lighting his retreat. He hurdled a fallen log, blocked branches with his forearm, and staggered in a downstream direction through the thicket of saplings. Terry picked up the .22, shook off the sleeping bag, and gave chase. The moonlight gave him a brief, clear shot. He aimed and fired.

The bullet ricocheted off a pine trunk a yard from Tom's head, striking him with bits of bark. Tom yelled, thinking he had been hit. He zigzagged as he ran. The temporary brightness gave him a course to follow even as clouds raced in once again to muffle the moonlight.

Terry stopped in the middle of their campsite. "Deke!" he shouted. "*Deke!* He's getting away!" Gail and Roarke sat bolt upright in their tent, both still bound in their sleeping bags. Gail saw Tom's bag was empty. She heard a second shot, then Deke's and Terry's frantic voices. "Tom?!" she shouted. "Tom, are you okay? Where are you?! Tom!!!"

Tom heard her voice and was driven to run even faster, branches slapping against his face. A branch scratched his eye, drawing tears. Momentarily disoriented, he caught his toe on a root and he went flying—*wunk*—landing facedown among the ground cover. The impact knocked his knife free. He fumbled in the dark to find it, on his knees, patting the earth here and there. His hand felt the steel blade. He grabbed the knife, snapped the blade shut, and jammed it in his pocket. Then he took off for the water's edge.

Terry raced to the perimeter of the campsite then stopped at the darkness, like a dog with an electronic collar remembering the pain zone beyond an invisible boundary. He squinted after Tom but could see nothing now; all he heard was a crashing in the thicket. Deke popped out of their tent and rushed up to him. "What happened?"

"He had a knife," Terry said. "Almost killed me. Son of a bitch."

"Why didn't you go after him?"

Terry stared at the darkness. "Out there? At night?"

"Where's your flashlight?" Deke asked.

"Lost it in the fight. I mighta hit him, Deke. I think I did. He yelled like I did."

"Chrissakes, gimme the gun. Keep an eye on the others." He ran back to their tent.

Gail and Roarke were cocooned in their sleeping bags in their tent. Gail eyed the cut lengths of rope around Tom's bag. "I snuck Dad my knife at the campfire," Roarke told her, proudly, eyes agleam. "He's going for help." Gail gave that some thought. The nighttime conditions, the enclosed canyon, Tom's urban instincts, the armed killers, the ingredients flashed through her mind in a blur of long odds and bad news. Gail smiled at her son. "I know he is."

** ** **

Deke scrambled out of the tent with a flashlight. He stopped beside Terry, who was still peering into the woods, trying to detect movement or sound. Terry pointed to a spot where spring runoff had thinned the new growth between the river's edge and the foot of the hills. "He headed down there. Unless he wants to go swimming, he ought to be pinned in by the canyon walls."

"It's time we had one less traveler," Deke said, clearly agitated to be dealing with a circumstance he thought was under control. He walked toward the water's edge, where he could follow the beach downstream, unimpeded until it gave way to new growth at the bottom of the run where canyon walls on both sides forced the River Wild through a kind of funnel.

Tom pushed through the cottonwood saplings that grew back from the river and were boxed in by the encroaching canyon. He paused to catch his breath, listen, and get his bearings. His eyes were beginning to adjust to the darkness. He could make out the looming form of the canyon wall that pinched in on him from river right. He could hear the roar of rapids he knew lay downstream of the tail-out. The glow of the campfire was faintly visible fifty yards upriver, like a lone firefly on a summer's night. He looked down to find himself standing in the soft mud of a spring whose flow originated somewhere back from the river in the run-up to the cliff. He followed the spring for a few yards until there was a clear pool to drink from. He knelt and cupped several handfuls of water. Then he made his way to the foot of the canyon wall and followed it to the river.

At the water's edge Tom paused to take stock. The far side of the river was bound by a towering sheer wall that matched the one on his side. Together, they forced the river into the mouth of a gorge between them, like the trickle point of an hourglass. Because of the narrowed width, the water ran swift, deep, and treacherous before giving way to a major rapids around the bend, where the canyon wall on Tom's side receded once more. Tom stepped into the river and peered downstream. He remembered Gail's description of the rapids being the roughest on the river outside of the Gauntlet. Survival seemed unlikely. The water dropped off quickly, the current was strong. With one more step, Tom found himself suddenly underwater—being swept toward the treacherous gorge. He bobbed to the surface and swam desperately toward shore. It took all his effort to get a toehold on the bottom. Just as quickly as he had lost his footing, he regained it and scrambled the short distance to shallow water, out of the current. He lay in the shallows until he caught his breath. The power of the river spooked him. He climbed back onto the shore.

What he saw next spooked him more: a flashlight beam piercing the darkness, moving toward him from the campsite. He glanced at the cliff wall across the river once more—no way out, even if he could get there. He walked to the base of the cliff on his side of the river and looked up: its granite surface gleamed in the light of a half-exposed moon. Up, up, up, it soared, its mostly smooth surface broken here and there by crevasses, ledges, and dwarf pine trees whose slender, twisted trunks angled out of cracks where windblown seeds had landed, taken root, and somehow survived. He stepped back far enough to glimpse the canyon rim a couple of hundred feet above, marked by a line of towering, dark pines. "*Oh, Tommmmm?*" Deke's voice, laced with a cat-and-mouse confidence, ended his deliberation.

Tom glimpsed the flashlight beam only thirty yards away now, lasering left and right through the scrub. For the first time, he could hear the rustle of the thicket above the whoosh of the river. Tom stared at the cliff once more; up was his only way out. He leaped for the root of a cliff-dwelling pine and grabbed it, adding a second hand to the first. His feet scrambled for a purchase on the cliff wall. He got enough leverage with his boots to pull himself up and reach one-handed for a second pine sapling a couple feet above the first. They all grew out of a vertical crevasse that offered a kind of wilderness ladder up to a ledge forty feet above the ground. The rough bark of the pines cut into Tom's hands, and his shoulders ached with the weight they were asked to support. But once he had navigated the first three or four limbs, he was able to stand on the lower saplings, taking the weight off his arms. It was faster going after that.

Deke, meantime, splashed into the muddy spring Tom had discovered. He held the flashlight in his left hand, the .22 in his right. He swung the light in a series of expanding arcs out from where he stood, training the gun wherever the beam alighted. Nothing. He aimed the flashlight on the muddy ground where he stood. He saw footprints, filling with water but still discernable. Deke stepped back to dry ground to better survey the mud. He knelt to inspect one of the prints. It was fresh, still holding its shape even filled with spring water. Deke traced them with the flashlight as they angled toward the river. Sensing he was closing in, he advanced in a stalking crouch, swinging the .22 one way then the other . . . pausing every few steps to listen. The sound of the river and the rapids below the gorge grew louder and louder.

Tom paused twenty feet above the ground to catch his breath. From his vantage he could see Deke's flashlight beam and even make out his form, edging toward the river. Tom looked around and knew he was a sitting duck if Deke saw him . . . at least until he made it to the ledge. His adrenaline surged. He reached for another pine and scrambled upward.

Deke emerged from the woods at the base of the cliff.

He knelt to inspect the boot prints once more. They led to the water's edge. Deke stepped cautiously into shallow water and aimed his flashlight at the facing cliff on the far side. He took another step deeper in and aimed the light downstream. The beam danced off the tops of white water churned by the beginning of the rapids. He took another step for a better angle and suddenly sank in waist deep. The current sucked at him. He found himself in that place fly fishermen have all encountered and forever wish to avoid: standing on the downslope of a gravel bed with diminishing traction and a fast current pushing at your back. He grunted in fear, desperate to avoid a second, likely fatal, trip through a River Wild rapids. He back-paddled with his arms and feet and slowly made his way to safer ground.

He splashed out of the water and stood at the base of the cliff, calculating his next move. A pebble bounced off his head. He stepped back and aimed his flashlight at the cliff wall, moving from one pine tree to another. The beam's brightness dissipated over distance, but was still able to illuminate Tom's boots forty feet up and the dark form of his body beyond.

Tom froze when the light hit him, but he quickly realized staying put was not an option. His fingers scratched at the granite and scrub growth in the crevasse above his head. He could see the ledge within reach, it was split by the vertical crevasse, making it easy to climb onto if he could get that far. Ironically, the flashlight beam revealed the nub of an old pine tree he hadn't seen. He pulled himself one-handed on the branch and inched his free hand upward toward the nub.

Below him, Deke smiled and shook his head. "I'll be goddamned." He tried to get a bead on Tom's body, but the steep angle made a good shot difficult. Deke backed up for a better perspective. When he reached the river's edge, he aimed his flashlight at the water's surface. He had a yard or two before the place where the current had gouged a dangerous drop-off.

Tom's boot toes scratched at the granite wall in an attempt to buy him another inch or two. His fingers hit the nub. He gripped it fully, and pulled with all his might, hoping to take advantage of the unexpected blackout. He reached his free hand above the nub and found another scrub pine. He tugged himself higher up the cliff, closer to the ledge.

Deke stepped as far into the river as he dared. He aimed the light once more at the darker, deeper water a foot behind him to get his bearings and know his limitations. He wiggled his feet into the river bottom for a more secure stance. He swung the flashlight beam onto the cliff. This time the light illuminated most of Tom's body, a dark form pressed to the lighter face of the granite wall.

Tom's head popped into view between the split halves of the ledge. It was a narrow passage. He was able to wiggle one elbow onto the ledge for leverage. He tried to pry himself through, but his shoulders and hips were too wide. He sunk back down and twisted his torso sideways.

Deke held his hands side by side, extended directly out from his body. One held the flashlight, the other the .22. He had shot enough to know a one-handed shot with a revolver at a sizable distance was a long shot at best. His trigger finger tightened; he was about to try a head shot, when Tom sank down. Deke decided a body shot was a better option. He squinted down the barrel and aimed for the crack in the ledge where Tom's body was now wedged. He pulled the trigger. The shot hit loose rock just below the ledge, inches from his target.

Tom kicked and pushed with his legs, finally twisting his body so that he fully faced one side of the ledge. He pressed his palms to the surface and pushed with all his might. He wiggled the top of his torso higher through the opening, but his hips got stuck. Tom's face contorted as he struggled to force his body through. "C'mon . . . c'mon!" A second shot ricocheted off the granite wall inches from his head, throwing chips against his face. "C'mon . . . fuck!" He realized he would have to somehow slide his body out of the crevasse to get it on the ledge. He pushed back from the wall with one hand as he kept an elbow crooked on the ledge. He inched his way free of the crevasse, and was half-on, half-off the ledge, both elbows on the rock, his legs dangling in space. He tried to surge forward on his elbows, but the depth of the ledge prevented his boots from getting a purchase on the wall. He needed one more handhold. A dwarf pine angled out of the cliff a yard away, just a foot above the ledge. Tom inched his way sideways.

Deke sidestepped slightly downstream for a better angle. His flashlight beam caught Tom half dangling from the ledge. Deke felt confident he had the shot. He transferred the butt of the flashlight to his mouth so he could hold the .22 two-handed. He wedged his feet against the river rocks to stabilize himself and trained the weapon on

Tom, whose white, bloodless hands the light caught gripping the ledge.

With his downstream hand, Tom reached out in a quick motion and got a hold of the pine, giving him enough leverage to pull himself up and over the ledge just as Deke fired. The shot hit the wall below the ledge, where Tom's legs had dangled a split second earlier. Tom screamed as he rolled his body against the face of the cliff on the yard-wide ledge. The shot dislodged a small rock, which freed a bigger one above it. The rocks sailed into space—their sudden absence loosening an even bigger boulder from the wall. The boulder—the size of a beer keg—sailed through the night air.

Deke stood twenty feet upstream of where the boulder *ker plunked* into the river. He swung his flashlight to the tail end of the dark, deep water that gave way to the top of the rapids. The light danced over the white froth of churned water. He thought he saw a dark form rise up once atop the surge, then sink from sight. Training the light once more at the ledge, he saw no movement and no sign of Tom. He raised the beam slightly, to see if Tom could have climbed upward. There was nothing but sheer wall.

Tom, on his back and pressed against the cliff, could see the beam of light angle above the ledge and illuminate the granite two yards above his head. If he had wanted to, he could have stuck his fingers in the light and made shadow puppets on the wall.

** ** **

Deke waded ashore, glanced once more at the cliff, and headed back to camp. Tom heard him in the thicket below. He flipped onto his stomach so he could peer over the ledge. He saw Deke's flashlight bouncing along the river's edge, where the walking was easier. Further off, the glow of the campfire made a yellow smudge in the blackness. Tom turned onto his back once more to survey the journey remaining: the massive slab of granite glistened in the moonlight, its surface pocked here and there by crevasses, stunted pines, and chutes. Way, way up—but closer now—the canopy of the canyon rim pines formed a green hedge as far as he could see up and downriver.

Deke walked out of darkness and found Gail and Roarke sitting around the fire, guarded by Terry. The fire blazed yellow, illuminating much of the campsite, fueled by a half dozen new logs.

"You get him?" Terry asked.

"I got him first, the fishies get him next," he said.

Gail gasped and pulled Roarke close against her.

Deke handed Terry the gun. "I'm going to get some dry clothes."

"Dad's dead, Mom?" Roarke looked at his mother with pleading eyes that suddenly burst into tears. "Did Deke kill him?"

"I don't know, honey." She hugged him fiercely. "I hope not."

Gail wrestled with the possibility that Deke was lying. She fought off an instinct to burst into tears, but she couldn't help a tear sliding from one eye. She felt queasy, churned by conflicting emotions. The lawyer in her cried out to wait for evidence. The layman in her clung to the last thing in her arsenal, hope. Her Ma Morgan membership hurried her momentarily past grief—there'd be time enough for that—to the more immediate prospect of revenge. But first she had to stay alive. The animal in her retreated to the most basic instinct: survival.

21

Mary K.'s gas station and convenience store sat on the banks of the Missouri River, upstream from the five consecutive waterfalls that gave Lewis and Clark a nineteen-day, nineteenth-century headache to portage around and the city of Great Falls its name. It occupied the no-man's-land just outside city limits en route to the checkerboard of ranches that filled most of Cascade County, including the abandoned ranch where Mary Walsh's red Ford sedan was found.

There was a pay phone by the front door, next to the ice cooler. Unlike old-fashioned pay phones elsewhere, it still got used. Among a clutter of signs and neon beer advertising in the window, one said: MINNOWS AND CRAWLERS FOR SALE. It was into this gas and food and beer lifeline that a Montana Fish and Game jeep pulled, canoe lashed on top. The ranger who got out was the one who had run into Gail and Tom on the river. His name was Thompson Littlebuck, and he was half Crow Indian, with jet-black hair and olive skin to prove it. He was twenty-nine. His cabin was two and a half miles upriver, making Mary K.'s oasis a kind of prime lie.

He stepped inside, through the screen door, past the fly strips dotted with the dried-out corpses of flies and the community bulletin board just inside the door. Country music played on an old plug-in radio. In the middle of a bunch of work-for-hire and wanted signs, there were mug shots of Deke and Terry. Mary K., the proprietor, greeted Thompson, a regular customer. True to her provocative nature, she wore a T-shirt that said "Free the Unabomber" and a black baseball cap with the white letters: FBI. She liked to explain the pairing was meant to indicate—in a humorous fashion—that one person's money was as good as another's at her establishment. "Evening, Thompson. The usual?"

"Better make it two quarts, Mary K. Been on the river too long." He glanced absently around the store as she collected the beer.

"Terrible thing about that Deer Lodge woman," she said, placing the beer in a brown bag.

"What happened?"

"The woman who was murdered. They found her car just up the road from Belt."

"I *have* been on the river too long. I figure I'll catch up with the news when I get home."

"Terrible thing," Mary K. said. "She seemed like such a nice person."

Thompson paid Mary Kent and gathered the cold

beer under his arm. The chill felt good against his body. "Doesn't get any better than this. See you when I see you."

"You know where I'll be," Mary K. said.

Thompson walked past the bulletin board with barely a glance. The screen door slammed behind him. Mary K. heard him climb into his jeep and close the door. She heard him turn on the ignition, then turn off the ignition. Next thing, Thompson Littlebuck practically burst through the screen door and fixed his eyes on Deke and Terry. "Holy shit."

22

Tom stood on a second narrow ledge, higher than the first that had saved his life. The clouds had parted, giving the full moon a chance to illuminate the task remaining. He stared up at a yard-wide chute that split the otherwise smooth granite wall and ran almost to the canyon rim. For an experienced free climber, it was an elevator to the top. For an architect from Brookline Village, it was a nightmare, albeit the best of the nightmares he had to choose from.

Tom stepped into the chute, which had a good yard's depth at this juncture. What he couldn't tell, and what he wouldn't know until he got there, was whether the chute remained deep enough for him to inchworm his way to the top. The width looked consistent, but the depth was harder to read as it approached the canyon rim. Truth be told, Tom wanted to cry, blink his eyes, and make everything go away—dismissed as a bad dream. But he was also a trained problem solver, something he reminded himself of to buoy his spirits. This was just another challenge. His past convinced him it was something he could do. Plus, he had a full tank of adrenaline to fuel the journey.

Tom flattened his back against one side of the chute and lifted one boot, then the other against the opposing side, so that his weight was suspended. He flattened his palms against the wall on either side of his butt. He experimented, pushing up with one hand, while creeping upward one boot sole at a time to a higher bracing. It worked. He inched his way up a few feet, then inched his way down, to plant his feet once more on the ledge and rest before launching the actual attempt. The model worked. Tom peeked out from the chute and glimpsed the diminished glow of the campfire to give him more incentive. "I love you," he whispered into the night air, in the direction of Gail and Roarke. Then he stepped back in and started up.

He realized about fifteen feet up that the varying width of the chute informed the degree of difficulty. When the chute narrowed, his knees almost touched his chest. It made breathing a little more forced, but it allowed him to rest his muscles more, too. When the chute widened and he had to use his thigh muscles to force his feet against the wall to create enough tension to hold himself in place, his muscles trembled with the effort and he had to fight off mini cramps. After ten minutes of climbing, he came to a narrower stretch, allowing him to rest. He looked up and down, and judged himself to be about halfway there. The depth of the chute proved consistent, which was encouraging, but his muscles were screaming for relief. He was sweating profusely with the exertion. His palms grew ever more slippery. His heart was thumping mightily.

When the moon ducked behind a new cloud cover, Tom's pale form made a ghostlike impression in the vertical shaft that appeared as a darker element in a dark-gray wall. With his scrunched posture, he also resembled a fetus in a birth canal. When the moon re-emerged, Tom glanced at the river. If his body hadn't been trembling and his limbs pulsing with fatigue, he would have enjoyed the play of moonlight on the river surface. The scuffed water of the rapids was brightening under the moon, while the darker, still pools hovered like floating ink spots against the sheer canyon wall.

Tom took a breath and pushed on. He could see the chute cleaving a final ledge he hadn't noticed from below, this one bristling with stunted pines and offering an easier path to the top. He inched his way toward the ledge. The width of the chute just below it widened slightly, which meant his muscles, which were losing resilience, had to work harder to maintain the tension between the parallel walls. When he got to the ledge, he reached up with his inside hand to find a good purchase. This put more strain on his wall-planted hand and the rest of his body, but it was a necessary outreach. Satisfied with his grip, he pushed back hard with his legs as he reached overhead with his other hand. He pulled his head over the ledge, pull-up–style, releasing the tension bond in the chute. It unnerved him to lose that safety position, and he sunk back so that he was once more wedged in the chute. He looked down. Because the cliff wall angled slightly back from the river, the chute appeared to fall away like a very steep, almost straight, bobsled run. Tom's toes began to quiver with the strain of holding him in place. He processed the information that the chute was a good foot wider at the top than at the bottom. His toes started to quiver faster and faster. His calves began to spasm. His body trembled with a final shudder to maintain its braced position—then his foot surrendered.

He cried out as he plunged downward. He knew if he lost full contact with the far wall, his descent would turn into a free fall and sure death. He pressed his palms against the wall on either side of his waist, even as he sought to maintain the fetal position that would eventually slow his descent when the chute narrowed. His shirt rode up as he plummeted down the coarse granite wall. It was like forcing himself over a cheese grater—his skin peeling off in sickening flecks. He screamed out.

He dropped forty feet before his bracing efforts and the narrowed chute slowed his fall. His body stopped two yards above the ledge from which he had started—his knees pressed almost to his chest, his boot soles flat against the far wall—his body wedged like a cork in a bottle. His hands and his back throbbed. His breathing came in compressed gulps. Below him, the first blood from his flayed back began to hit the ledge in little splatters. The drops came faster and faster as the blood seeped out of his abraded back and followed gravity downhill. Tom closed his eyes. This time he allowed himself to cry.

** ** **

Gail's eyes popped open in her dark tent. She wasn't sure when she had fallen asleep; the overload of bad news and bad scenarios had finally short-circuited her brain and she had gone black. But now she was sure there was something wrong in her space. A form loomed over her. All at once, Terry's face was inches from hers, his breath redolent of whisky. Gail yelped. Her body tightened.

"Mom?" Roarke's anxious, small voice pierced the blackness.

Terry clamped a huge hand over Gail's mouth. It covered her like a surgeon's mask, revealing only her eyes, shimmering with fear. He moved his other hand down her sleeping bag, groping her between her legs. Gail struggled, but Terry pressed his substantial weight onto her, pinning her to the ground. He leaned even closer to smell her, his hand still covering her mouth

"Mom?" Roarke sat up in the darkness, his pale face visible in the oval of his bound, blue mummy sack. The sight of his mother being violated, on top of the specter of his father's death overwhelmed him. He cried and yelled out at the same time, "Get off her! Leave her alone!" He struggled to loosen or break his restraining rope.

Terry glared at the boy and pushed him roughly. "Shut the fuck up." Roarke tumbled into the side of the tent. Terry returned his gaze to Gail. His eyes undressed her. The thought of Gail naked filled his face with an ecstatic leer. His expression changed when he felt the barrel of a .22 pressed to the side of his head. He slowly rolled off Gail and confronted Deke, glaring at him. "The fuck's the matter with you?"

"She gives me a bone."

"The *fucking knotty pine* gives you a bone." Deke

tapped Terry's forehead with the gun barrel. "You gotta start thinking more with this head."

"You just want her for yourself."

"You're dumber than river rocks," Deke told him. "Don't you get it? Leave her fucking alone until she gets us off this river. Is this so fucking hard to understand?!

After the fucking rapids you can do what you want to her. Fuck her in the trees. Fuck her in the water. Fuck her to death if you want. But just leave her *a-fucking-lone* till then!"

Terry glared at Deke before skulking off. Deke looked at Gail, cowering in her sleeping bag. He touched the barrel of his .22 to his forehead pretending to tilt up the brim of a Stetson in the traditional cowboy gesture: *At your service, ma'am.* Deke climbed out of the tent and zipped the front flap shut behind him.

Roarke rolled next to his mother. His face was wet with tears. "You okay, Mom?"

"He didn't do anything," Gail told him. She rolled onto her side so they were face to face in their bound sleeping bags. She kissed him and moved her head lovingly against his. "Are *you* okay?"

"I can't believe Dad's . . . dead." He heaved out the words between deep sobs.

Gail pulled her face back far enough to look him in the eyes. "I don't think he is," she whispered.

"You're just saying—"

"No. I mean it. In my gut I think he's alive. My gut's pretty truthful."

Roarke's eyes sparkled with hope. "Really?"

"Really. Dad's okay." She managed a smile. "You'll see. . . . *We'll* see."

** ** **

A sad-eyed Maggie stared down from the canyon rim at the remaining red glow of the campfire. She rested her muzzle on her crossed paws as dogs do. She whimpered, got up and paced a few feet away and collapsed in a heap once more, muzzle upon paws.

Not a quarter mile away, Tom inched his way downriver along the ledge. It turned a corner with the wall, where the sheer face started to recede from the river's edge. Tom made it as far as the ledge went. From this new vantage, he could look below to where the rapids gave way to the next long run. Just off the ledge, a crevasse angled up, filled with soil, pebbles, and several stunted pines. More promising, it led to another, wider shelf that led to a trail that angled upward toward the rim, like a ramp. The problem was getting there.

Tom removed his knife, opened the sturdy can-opener blade and began cleaning out the pebbles that clogged the lower portion of the crevasse in reach. All he needed was one good handhold to get to the lowest pine— that led to a succession of handholds, which led up to the broad shelf. Satisfied with his housekeeping, Tom closed and pocketed his knife. He pressed his body flush to the cliff wall and reached out with his left hand. He groped in the crevasse until his hand found a suitable nub to hold onto. He gauged the distance once more from that hand-hold to the pine above. It seemed reachable; in Tom's judgment, a better option than returning to the chute. He waited for the moon to come out once more, and to work up the nerve. The whole surface of his back throbbed with the kind of penetrating pain a severe burn generates. If his brain wasn't focused on an even more powerful force—survival—he might have surrendered and lay down in a heap.

When the moon was revealed behind the racing clouds, Tom reached out once more and grabbed the nub. He took a breath and leaned off the ledge, as gently as he could. His body swung into space, seventy-five feet above the rapids. His feet scratched for support to relieve the weight on his left arm and shoulder as his right hand joined his left in the crevasse, groping for a suitable grip. He was glued to the wall in four points. He looked up and eyed the pine limb he had to reach. He pulled with his left hand and stabbed his right hand upward. It fell inches short of the pine and the momentum of the effort collapsed his body once more to the first, dangling position. Tom groaned. There was little strength left in his left arm and hand—enough for one more try. He returned his right hand to the crevasse to relieve some of the weight on his left side. He gathered himself for a do-or-die leap. He began rocking his body gently against the wall once, twice, like a kid on a swing trying to get higher. On the third swing, Tom launched himself upward. His toes scratched for even the smallest purchase. He pulled down with all his might, his right hand slapped overhead, and his fingertips grazed the limb. He groaned and willed another inch of trajectory. His right hand settled around the limb, which bent with the weight, but held. He released his left hand, shook it out once, then swung it overhead for a two-handed grip on the pine. The little tree creaked beneath his full weight, and a handful of dirt and pebbles popped out of the crevasse. The root mass pulled slightly out, spilling more dirt, but held. Tom knew time was of the essence. He planted both feet against the granite wall, and surged upward once more. He reached the second stunted pine and then the third, which allowed him to step onto the upper ledge.

He sank to all fours on the wide ramp. His arms throbbed. His back was on fire. He puked with the exertion. He lowered his head into his hands. When he was rested, he scrambled up the gently sloped stone ramp and disappeared into a cavelike opening. It was pitch black until the moon shone bright once more—visible in the open-air lid carved out of the cavern ceiling. Tom easily climbed over the rounded boulders that time had eroded and left like a stack of cannon balls just below the canyon rim. Pine trees stood at the edge of the void, their roots poking through the thin topsoil like old, gnarled fingers. The ground was coated with pine needles. The night was pine scented. Tom looked down at the River Wild—a silver ribbon far below. He peered downstream, where he knew he had to go. In the dark, the surrounding mountains looked soft and almost rounded. Way beyond, at the farthest place his eyes could see, the lights of Great Falls glimmered like a bed of scattered coals.

23

Tom might have taken heart if he had known that somewhere in that urban bed of scattered coals State Police Detective Lieutenant Bobby Long was looking in his exact direction, on a map. Ranger Thompson Littlebuck stood to one side. Trooper Billy Heston hovered nearby. The clock on the wall indicated it was a little before midnight. Littlebuck pointed to a location on the River Wild. "This is where I saw them."

The lieutenant held up mug shots of Deke and Terry. "These guys? William Patterson and Terrance O'Reilly."

"Those two, positively. Plus a couple and their kid. The husband's face was a mess. They must have beat the shit out of him. He told some story about getting tossed out of the boat in the rapids, but you don't look like that . . . plus, now that I think about it, his wife said she was a guide, so I doubt he would've gotten tossed with her rowing—if she was rowing . . ." He paused to remember. "The big guy, Terry, had the kid off to a distance. That was pretty weird. But when you're trying to get off the river and you've talked to fifty campers, it doesn't register as it does now, when you have time to think about it."

"You think they were gonna spend the night there?"

"Looked like it," Littlebuck said. "Plus it was pretty late in the day. They were all soaked. It's a moderately rough stretch of water they came through."

"How far from there to takeout?"

"About eight miles."

The lieutenant studied the map below the campsite. "What's the last part of the river like?"

The ranger traced the final segment down to the take-out. "You've got four miles of slow water and steep canyon below them. Then there's Indian Gorge, the toughest rapids on the river, except for the Gauntlet, which nobody runs. Least, nobody sane. Below Indian Gorge, you've got some gentle meadowland, then you hit the last two miles of canyon and you're out."

The lieutenant's wheels were turning. It was the lead he needed—the addition of luck that sometimes rewarded good police work. Bobby Long burned brightly with new energy and ideas. Standard procedure would likely still win the day, but for the first time, intuition took the lead. "You ever been down the Gauntlet?" he asked Littlebuck.

The ranger smiled. "Not all us Indians are drunk and crazy."

The lieutenant smiled. "You know anybody who has?"

"A few guides and white water hounds. It's about as challenging a descent as you'll find in the States."

"You said the woman was a guide."

"That's what she told me, before she was married."

"Think she's ever been down the Gauntlet?"

Thompson shrugged. "Not recently, I don't imagine."

"Did you get her name, by any chance?"

"Gail, something," Littlebuck said. He paused to think, shook his head. "I meet a lot of people."

"Think hard," the lieutenant said. "It could be important."

"I remember she gave me her married name and then . . . as I'm remembering it now, she gave me her maiden name. Didn't seem weird then, but maybe she was trying to pass information to me."

"*Gail's* not going to do it."

"What did she look like?" Heston asked.

"Blond. In her forties. Attractive . . . though on the river people tend to let go.

"Definitely fit."

"How tall?"

"Five six, five seven, maybe. Their son could have been ten to fourteen, I guess. The other guy, Terry, had him off at a distance."

"That's something we might be able to work with," the young trooper told him.

"She mentioned she'd been down the river a million times," Littlebuck added.

"So someone's going to know her," Heston said, hopefully. "I checked with Fish, Wildlife, and Parks. It's a river you have to win a lottery to get on. Lot of the same outfitters specialize in running it—some of them with an annual permit allotment. If she's been on it a lot, she was probably with one of the major outfitters. That's easy to check."

"One of the names was Anderson," Littlebuck blurted, "though I can't remember if that was the married or maiden name. I think she said it second, which would have been the maiden name."

"So, this Gauntlet . . . it's doable?" Bobby Long asked.

"Doable?" Littlebuck snorted. "Let's say people have done it. Bunch more drowned *trying* to do it."

The lieutenant pointed to the logging road that switch-backed into the river below the Gauntlet. "You ever get to the river on this road?"

"Couple times. The stretch below isn't as beautiful as the stretch above . . . or as long, but a few folks like to put in there and take it all the way to the Missouri. It doesn't get fished as hard."

"Let's go back to the last takeout before the Gauntlet. Show me where that is, exactly."

"Right here. Canyon Gorge. The cliffs rise up kind of like gates and that's it."

"Say these guys, for obvious reasons, weren't plan-ning to let that family go at the takeout. After she got them through the rapids. Say they were going to leave them," he grimaced, "one way or the other above the takeout. Where would be the best place to get some men in?" Littlebuck pointed to the meadows below Indian Gorge.

"This would be the easiest place onto the river itself. Only problem is there're no road in."

"Helicopter?" Billy Heston piped up.

"You could," the lieutenant said, "but if those sons of bitches see or hear a chopper, you'd be looking at a family with a diminished life expectancy. Not that they're gonna let them go anyway."

"You know these guys?" Littlebuck asked.

Bobby Long looked haunted. "Yeah, I know one of them." Billy Heston took note of the lieutenant's demeanor; he had never seen him stone-faced like this.

The ranger pointed to the cliffs just above the takeout. "There's a fire road into here. Piece of cake for four-wheel drive. But getting down those cliffs would be something else."

Long gave that some thought. "If you can get me in there," he said, determined, "I'll round up some men who'll get down."

"Sir?" Billy Heston bravely ventured another suggestion. "You might want some sort of disguises."

"Such as?"

"Fishing stuff?"

Long looked at Heston in a new light. "I'll buy that," he said. "We'll need the help of a fishing shop."

"It's midnight sir, and Sunday, to boot."

"Trooper, I don't give a flying fuck if it's Christmas and St. Patty's Day rolled into one. Get someone up, and get one of those shops open."

Billy Heston said, "No problem, sir."

He stood there for the longest moment, as if that was that. The lieutenant gave him a look. "No time like the present."

"Yes, sir." Billy started for the door. "Trooper, I also

want you to ask around the fishing shops and see what anyone remembers about a guide named Gail Anderson. Dig
up as much background as you can, wherever you can. Do
that Google shit, too."

"Yes sir," Billy said, "I'll do the Google shit."

The lieutenant turned once more, to study the map.
His gut was talking to him.

** ** **

Billy Heston's fingers flew over his computer keyboard.
Maybe all the stupid video games and "computer bullshit"
his father always harped on when Billy was trying to survive Montana winters had an upside after all. "Montana
Outfitters, Great FallsArea," turned up six company names
and numbers. He was ready for some after hours "if this is
an emergency" phone numbers and calls.

** ** **

In his office, Bobby Long was working the phones. "Jared,
it's Bobby. Yes, I know what time it is. Time for you to get
your ass to the mother ship. We got a bead on the bad guys.
Round up the boys. Full tactical gear. Zero dark thirty." He
hung up and sat back in his chair. He flashed on the police
photograph of his wife's best friend and maid of honor,
Mary Walsh, eyes wide, neck broken. He sat still for the
longest time, visibly haunted.

** ** **

The web site for Montana Troutfitters popped up on the screen. Billy Heston bypassed the "grip and grin" snaps of happy clients holding trout and down to the list of company guides. He hurried past the younger ones and wrote down the names of the older guides. He did the same for three more fishing outfitters, then started dialing.

24

Gail and Deke faced each other across the fire, captive and captor, looking every bit the chess players they were—silently plotting their next moves, trying to think a move or two ahead. Gail's hands were bound.

"I need to pee," Gail said.

Deke got up and untied her. "*Roarke* says you got two minutes."

Gail headed for the woods between the campsite and the rafts.

She looked back when she was far enough in to be unseen. The fire was an orange blur. She pulled out a spool of monofilament fishing leader from her shirt pocket. She glanced around, her eyes darting from tree to tree, searching, searching, settling finally on two saplings three feet apart. A splintered tree stump with a nasty jagged tip formed the third point of a triangle, half a body length away from the trees. Gail crouched down and tied the open end of the line to one of the saplings, shin high, then looped the spool around the other tree, shin high, repeated the process two more times to strengthen the bridging linkage, and wove the last length around the six strands to bundle them together.

Deke's voice reached her, "Ten-second warning! Nine ... eight ... "

Gail quickly bit off the monofilament and worked to secure it to one of the trees. Her guide's hands remembered their old dexterity, working furiously and efficiently to tie off the line as she had so many clients' flies.

** ** *

A mile downriver, Tom ran through the woods at the rim of the canyon. He would gauge his path and make hay when the moon was exposed, slow down when cloud cover dimmed the light. He wasn't sure where he was going, except downriver ... where everyone he cared about was headed. He paused every now and then when a vista opened to peer into the distance, hoping to see a possible way down to the river's edge. A place where he could fashion a rescue or ambush of some kind. Those details would have to wait. First he needed a site and a way to it.

He scrambled up a gentle, pine needle–covered slope and paused at the top to assess the short leap to the ground below. Not bad. He jumped and landed softly in a bed of needles. He stood to brush off his palms and chart the next leg forward. He heard a low *growl*. Spooked, Tom turned to see a grizzly sow surge out of the cavern formed by the underside of the slope. The bear charged closer, then reared back on hind legs, fangs bared, saliva dripping from her gums. She clawed the air with her paws, hissed and roared. Tom screamed and threw up a protective forearm. He instinctively staggered backward. The bear scrambled even closer, slashing her paws through the night air, inch-long claws looking like talons—black against cinnamon-colored paws. Tom stumbled away. His heel hit a rock and down he went in a heap. The bear reared up directly above his prostrate form, snorting and hissing, the gobs of saliva now dripping from her jaw like live stalagmites. Tom could smell her putrid breath. A snarling, golden blur hurtled out of the darkness from the side. Maggie slammed into the bear, grabbing a mouthful of coarse fur from the sow's throat. The dog's momentum knocked both creatures to the ground. The unexpected attack startled the sow more than anything. Maggie tumbled free when they both hit the ground. She pounced to her feet and confronted the bear head on, barking as ferociously as a golden retriever could. The bear scrambled to all fours and kind of backed up to assess the situation. A new adversary changed her thinking, especially since her goal was to protect her young cubs, who now wandered out of darkness and head-bumped her backside. The sow turned on the cubs and sent them scrambling backward with a hiss threatening punishment.

Tom took the opportunity to roll further away from the bear and scramble to higher ground. Maggie continued to bewilder the bear with her barking and feints. The sow finally had enough. She rose up on her haunches and made herself as tall as she could. She roared and hissed again and sliced her paws through the air. Maggie sensed her work there was done. She bolted.

Tom, meantime, had scrambled to the top of the next knoll downriver. "Maggie!! Come on, girl!"

The bear took a couple of steps toward the departing dog, then stood a final time. Tom had no doubt she would kill them both if they didn't disappear and stop threatening her offspring.

When Maggie bounded up to him, Tom draped an arm over her neck, then stood and started running. The sow retreated to the shelter of her cavern.

Tom ran until he thought it was safe to stop in an opening on the canyon rim. He sank to his knees to catch his breath and hug his dog. Maggie slobbered him with licks and kisses, squirming in his arms. Tom buried his head in Maggie's fur. At last, an ally. The reunion was joyful, if brief. Tom knew he had to hurry and find a way down to the river's edge; time was short. But, as far as he could see, on his side of the river there were only the vertical plates of canyon walls.

** ** **

And so, when the near-full moon splashed enough light through the pine trees to safely read the terrain, he began running again. At full wattage, the moon was bright enough to cast shadows. In places where the forest thickened, he veered back toward the canyon rim, where tree growth was usually less because the winter winds howled over the edge and blew away topsoil, leaving little nourishment. Maggie ran with him; each was happy for the other's company. In time, Tom found a rhythm he remembered as a kid, running with his springer spaniel after school in the woods behind his house in Connecticut. Only where the trees grew close together did he have to slow to a walk and skip through the clutter of trunks that were packed, in places, as tightly as a fistful of pick-up sticks.

Tom returned to the canyon rim at intervals to check his progress and gauge where he had to go. He figured the likeliest place to find a way down was somewhere below the rapids at Indian Gorge, the place Gail had talked about. He knew that was the last tricky run before the takeout. It would be his best shot at some sort of ambush or rescue. He checked the cloud cover as often as the river. The combination of low light and dense tree growth made for the worst progress; full moon and open, wavelike undulations of granite allowed him to make good time.

He paused at an open bluff to catch his breath. The moon, unfiltered by clouds, shone its light into the gorge and onto the froth of rapids Tom figured must be Indian Gorge. They looked magical from above, a long patch of churned water between deeper, darker markings of slower water upstream and down. The canyon rim was high here— a good half mile above the river, with sheer cliff walls—but the acoustics of the rapids added a gentle rush he heard for the first time. Bathed in moonlight, the enveloping wilderness took on a pristine and serene glow—a magical quality Gail had long savored and lovingly described.

Tom had seen enough of the river and its geologic rhythm to know that it was corseted in places by steep, facing canyon walls that gave way to cliffs on one side and more gentle—climbable—slopes on the other. Being on the cliff side of Indian Gorge, there was no path to the water's edge. He spied another open promontory about a mile downstream from where he stood. It was below the Indian Gorge rapids and offered a good vantage of the river from which he could watch Gail tackle the white water. The problem was he would only be a spectator; there was no way down. No matter, there was no alternative other than to be there. He rubbed Maggie on her golden dome and began running once more.

25

Morning light grew incrementally brighter at the river's edge. The charcoal of night turned lighter, then grayer, then a lighter shade of gray, then dirty white, then a brighter shade of white as the sun rose higher in the sky and its rays penetrated deeper into the canyon. Fog hung over the water in gossamer patches. Terry loaded the tents and other camp gear into the beached raft. Deke oversaw a somber breakfast for Gail and Roarke that consisted of cold cereal. When they were finished, he told them it was time to move on. He stood back to shepherd them to the raft. Gail took Roarke's hand and suddenly made a run for the woods, tugging the boy with her.

"Goddamnit, Gail," Deke shouted after. He shook his head, then snatched the .22 from his belt and gave chase.

"C'mon, honey, faster!" Gail challenged Roarke. She glanced back to make sure Deke was following. She crashed through a small bush at the edge of the campsite and scrambled toward a stand of trees. She headed toward two saplings only a yard's-width apart. At the last moment, she veered around them, and sprinted toward a clearing at the foot of the steep, grassy hill that led out of the canyon. Deke quickly closed the gap. He realized he could cut them off by angling through the trees. He smiled, enjoying the pursuit.

When he sprinted between the trees his shins hit the nearly invisible monofilament tripwire Gail had tied in place the night before. His momentum sent him sprawling headfirst into the splintered stump of a tree that Gail had figured into her trap. *WUNK*—Deke hit the ground hard and lay still—his gun hand stretched out before him, the tip of the stump poking through his shirt.

Gail skidded to a halt. She waited a moment. Deke didn't move. She peered through the brush, toward the water. Terry was leaning into the raft, adjusting something, preoccupied. Gail stared at Deke's motionless body and swallowed. She left Roarke and hurried toward the .22. As she knelt to reach for the weapon, Deke raised it from the forest floor and aimed at Gail. His head was next, angling upward. Gail froze. The barrel of the .22 was pointed at her midsection.

Deke locked eyes with Gail, then slowly pushed himself back onto his knees. A splinter from the stump had passed between his arm and his chest, where it missed doing any serious damage. He inspected the torn shirt and a slight skin wound: a little blood but nothing dire.

He turned to look at the monofilament tripwire, then back at Gail. He shook his head. "Darlin', you're something." His voice was filled with admiration. "If I ever need a killer lawyer . . ."

** ** **

Terry stroked the raft away from the campsite. Deke was in the bow; Gail and Roarke were huddled in the back, tied to D rings. Terry made his way to the main current, then swung the bow downstream as Gail had taught him. At the bottom of the run, they passed beneath the cliff Tom had scaled the night before. Gail and Roarke eyed the sheer wall: the first ledge and then the second ledge with the chute above. Their gazes finally made it to the top of the canyon and the green line of towering pines that hugged the rim. Fully illuminated by morning sun, the entirety of the massive facade revealed itself like a giant relief map. Roarke stared at the cliff dull-eyed, numbed by the improbability of it being his father's escape route. Deke taunted them by removing his .22, aiming it at the cliff and pretending to shoot. He blew imaginary smoke from the barrel and returned the gun to his belt.

Tears fell from Gail's eyes. She pulled Roarke closer to her. "Don't worry, honey, Dad's gone for help," she whispered.

"Wasn't any room for him anyway," Deke said, matter of fact.

The raft floated around the bend, dipped into faster water, and disappeared.

** ** **

Set back from the north rim of the canyon, the pine forest gave way to an alpine meadow carpeted with wild flowers.

The gentle morning hush of wilderness yielded to the faint sound of something man-made. A mechanical drone, at odds with the pristine surroundings, grew louder and was swelled by the ebb and flow of car engine acoustics—now clearly decipherable. A ranger's Fish and Game jeep burst out of the woods at the edge of the meadow. The first jeep was followed by a second, third, and fourth, all marked with Montana State Police logos and lettering. The final vehicle to emerge from the woods and make its way across the meadow was a van with the words BEAR CANYON ANGLERS visible on the sides and hood.

Thompson Littlebuck drove the lead vehicle. Rodeo veteran Bobby Long rode shotgun. His large body barely moved as his legs absorbed the bumps and sways of the uneven terrain. "How much further?" he asked Littlebuck.

"We're almost there," Littlebuck said. "Far end of the meadow."

** ** **

Ten minutes later, the ranger and the lieutenant stood near the edge of the towering cliff overlooking Indian Gorge and the rapids below. Long had traded his police uniform for cowboy boots, blue jeans, and a Western-style snap-button field shirt. He scanned the river with a pair of binoculars, then lowered the glasses and shook his head.

"This is the next-to-last stretch after the rapids, before the takeout," Littlebuck explained. He carved an S in the air for the lieutenant as he pointed downriver.

"Maybe two miles from here . . . after the second linked meander. Then, you see where the cliffs narrow?"

Long trained his binoculars downriver. "Yeah."

"That's Canyon Gorge takeout. The river gets squeezed between cliffs just downstream from there, generating this incredible surge that hurtles you into the big one—the Gauntlet."

Bobby Long lowered his glasses and stepped up to the edge of the cliff. He took in the hundred yard sheer drop to the water below, then squinted into the distance to the Gauntlet and beyond, where the mountains and the canyons crowded together, folding the river in their midst, seeming to form a single tapestry of wilderness beneath a piercing blue sky. "One hell of a river, tell you what," he said to the ranger.

"Oh, yeah," Thompson Littlebuck said. "This one named itself."

Behind the two men, a half dozen state troopers, recruited from a special SWAT unit, were gearing up. The men, dressed in commando fatigues, lugged coils of rope from the jeeps to the sheer drop. One end of each coil was anchored to a tree trunk or rock. Elsewhere, sharpshooters staked out shooting stations along the canyon rim, each man positioned by a supervising trooper to cover a certain stretch of the river. At the Bear Canyon Anglers van, the commandos were handed wading boots, fishing vests, and pack rods by the store owner—civilian ingredients first. The men stuffed the gear into backpacks before stopping at the arms vehicle to collect the business end of their equipment: knives, handguns, and ammunition.When the men were fully provisioned, they gathered around Bobby Long for final instructions. "Take up positions one bend below Indian Rapids. In your fishing gear. It's possible the suspects will row straight to the takeout with the hostages, but that seems unlikely. The woman's a former river guide. One scenario has her getting them through the rapids, the last tricky stretch before the takeout. After that, her value to them goes down. Which is where you come in . . . and why you're going to be where you are. They snapped that Red Lodge woman's neck. They might have killed others. Mr. Littlebuck here said it looked to him that they had beaten the shit out of the husband. Who knows if they've done something worse since. We want you to make sure no one else gets killed . . . unless it's these two guys."

Long held up mug shots of Deke and Terry. "I don't much care if they come off the river in a body bag. But I want the woman, her husband, and the boy alive. You're in fishing gear to give you the element of surprise. They don't know we know they're on the river, at least we *think* they don't. They're no doubt armed. If you can somehow separate them from the family members—*safely*—fine. If there's any question, shoot first. Is that clear? You'll have sharpshooter backup, but you're Plan A. First interceptors. We don't know when they'll be coming downriver, but our assumption is sometime in daylight. Any questions?"

"I can't fish for shit," one of the SWAT members offered.

The ranger laughed. "Believe me, you won't be the first floater on this river who can't fish."

"Besides, you're not fishing for fish," Bobby Long reminded him. "And this ain't *catch and release*. All you gotta do is *look* like a fisherman. Dick around with your gear, peer into your fly box, untangle a line snarl, catch your fly in a tree—do what most fishermen do. Anyone else?" Silence. "Radios don't work for shit in the canyon, so once you're down there you're on your own. Which means I expect you to use your judgment and do what you have to do. Okay? Good luck."

The men walked to the three coils of rope and hurled them over the cliff. They buckled their rappeling belts in place and secured the rope in their belt rings.

They tightened their backpack straps a final time. One by one, they pushed off from the edge of the rim and sailed out over the river. They paid out line as gravity took hold, pushing off from the canyon wall when the arc of their descent swung them back into the rock face at the end of each line release.

** ** **

Across from the SWAT team, but upriver one bend and unaware of their presence, Tom and Maggie settled into a vantage point that offered a view of Indian Gorge rapids. There was no way down; the cliffs were sheer. There was a sandy beach at the tail end of the rapids, before the river slalomed once more out of sight, where the SWAT team would take up their positions. Tom wrestled with the reality that Gail had no reason to believe he was alive. He remembered their conversation when they were alone in the raft: Gail's haunting decision to proactively flip the raft even if it meant their deaths. *If it really gets down to it, I'd rather nobody got off this river alive.* Tom knew his wife well enough to know she meant it. If there were no other options.

He touched his head to Maggie's. "She doesn't know we're alive; neither of us."

He looked around and saw a tree he could climb. He made his way to the lone pine and jumped to reach the first branch. The rest was easy, a series of almost alternating branch steps. He held on tight just below the very top. The trunk swayed with his weight. The river was even more distant. Tom looked upriver first, then down. What he saw was a river bed that made a huge U at Canyon Gorge and reversed course. There were S turns along the way, but they were the smaller elements of a larger course change. The corseting walls in the middle of the Gauntlet were the pivot point. Tom traced the river up to and after that landmark. If for any reason he needed to get to the river below the Gauntlet, there was a very short leg, not following the canyon rim, but cutting across and in effect closing the distance between the points of the larger horseshoe.

** ** **

Detective Lieutenant Long's next stop was downstream at Canyon Gorge takeout. Dozens of cars, many with trailers, were parked in the dirt parking lot that stretched back from the takeout ramp. A half dozen Montana state trooper vehicles were also visible. Troopers—wearing shorts and river sandals, as instructed—unloaded the gear. Handguns were inspected and placed out of sight in back-packs. A couple of troopers set up tents. Extra ammunition and other weapons were stored inside, out of sight.

Trooper Page Noel reported to the lieutenant. "Get these vehicles out of sight as soon as you can," Long told him.

"We're spooking some of the campers, lieutenant. They want to know what's going down."

"Tell them it's just a training exercise. *Spooking the bad guys* is the only thing worries me."

The two troopers walked to the water's edge as a raft pulled in and a family of four raised their paddles in cele-bration. They were met by grandparents, who grabbed the nose of the Avon and pulled it onto the ramp. Hugs and whoops and excited children's voices ensued.

The troopers walked upstream, out of earshot.

"Everybody's in position," Long told Noel. "You're the belt. The suspenders are about two miles upstream."

"What does that make you, Lieutenant?"

"Insurance," Bobby Long said. "That thing you pay for every year and never use until you need it. That's me. Let's move those vehicles out."

Noel hurried off. Long walked to a horse trailer hitched to a pickup truck near the back of the lot. A horse's tail fluttered out of the open back end. Long reached in and rubbed Marlene's nose. He reached into a pocket for a carrot and offered it to the horse. "Keep your strength up, girl. You're my insurance."

"Lieutenant!" Trooper Heston rushed up and held

out a piece of paper. "That woman you wanted me to find out about . . . Gail Anderson. That *was* her maiden name. Married Tom MacDonald, a Boston architect. I talked to a couple of fishing shops, then to a handful of clients who used her. Turns out she was a pistol in her day. A little headstrong, maybe, but nothing but rave reviews. Daughter of a rancher. Best female fisherman by far. Hell of a rower. Had a number of first descents out west and in the Andes. *Kicked field goals for the Cascade boys' high school football team!* Basically, the girl kicked ass."

Bobby Long studied the assessment for a moment. "Good," he said, visibly pleased with her country pedigree. "Let's hope she left something in the tank for two more."

26

Gail back-rowed at the tail end of the run upriver of the Indian Gorge rapids. She wanted to buy time to plot her course through the white water. She had run it dozens of times, years ago, but each time, she knew, was always different—depending on water flow and any shifting of rocks and channels that inevitably happened every year during runoff. What she saw was a hundred yards of chop and froth pinched between towering canyon walls. She back-oared once, twice, slowing the raft in the tail out. She stood up to peer downstream. Like a high jumper charting her approach to the bar, she mentally broke down her route into manageable pieces. Satisfied at last, she sat once more and adjusted her line. "Hold on, Roarke" she said. He was seated behind her, beside Terry. Deke was in the bow. He slid off the seat and onto the bottom of the raft. He gripped the canvas handles in either hand.

The raft hurried out of the fast-moving, shallow tail-out and into the first churn of the rapids. The nose immediately shot up and smacked down with a splash. Water surged over the bow, soaking Deke. Gail back-oared to line up the first chute, then swung the bow straight downriver and accelerated their speed with a two-oar push. The raft split two rocks and sank into a chute bounded by white water on either side. Gail abruptly swung the blades of her oars out of the water and thrust her hands forward to swing the blades over either side of the raft to avoid banging her oars on the rocks.

When she passed through the rocks, she swung the oars back into action, back-paddling to river right to avoid a reeflike island in the middle of the river where a log had lodged itself. She rose out of her seat with the exertion. The raft hurtled toward the log on a three-quarters slant. When Gail was satisfied she had bought enough space to clear the obstacle, she jammed her left oar into the current and pulled hard on the right to center the raft once more. The Avon sailed past and under one end of the log that angled out from the rocks. Deke had to flatten himself to the raft floor to avoid being hit. It all happened in the blink of an eye. He turned to glower at Gail once they shot by. The close call gave Gail an idea.

The river bent slightly to the right ahead, forcing a good tongue of water against the outer cliff wall. She scrambled with the oars to aim her butt river left, and pulled for all she was worth to make the far chute. She turned to Roarke and screamed, "Hold on!" then she rose up for even more leverage. The raft edged closer to the canyon wall. At the bottom of the chute Gail saw a rock punch through the surface maybe eight feet off the cliff face.

** ** **

Tom watched her from a quarter mile away. He was lying on his stomach on a flat shelf over a sheer drop that afforded him a fishbowl vantage of Indian Gorge rapids. It was like watching a hockey game from peanut heaven: the specifics were unclear, but the shape of play, the spacing of the elements, and the view of the whole venue offered a unique perspective on what was unfolding. He could see the route choices Gail turned down, and the degree of difficulty in the path she had chosen. It was a tight fit between the cliff wall and the rock that geysered a spigot of water off its top. He watched Gail center herself in the main current. At the last moment, as the raft rushed toward the wall and the rock, Tom watched Gail angle the nose of the raft slightly river right.

** ** **

Deke, facing forward, peered over the bow as the raft gathered speed and was sent hurtling downstream by the tongue of current. The bow drifted river right as they attempted to split the distance between the rock and the cliff wall. Gail gave one last back tug on her right oar—unseen by Deke. The right side of the raft's bow crashed into the rock, then rose up and over it . . . . the force of the collision throwing Deke violently to his left, prying his handhold off the right canvas strap. The collision also ricocheted the bow river left. Moments later, the raft, almost broadside in the current, slammed into the cliff wall. Gail reinforced the crash with a two-handed thrust of the oars. Deke was catapulted out of his hunkered-down position. His body hit the wall as water poured into the raft, then it slipped into the water as the collision—and subsequent "springing effect" of the raft's tube structure—opened a gap between the raft and the cliff. Deke held fast with his left hand and managed to get a two-handed grip on the canvas strap. Gail stood and jammed her left oar into the current, throwing the nose once more against the cliff. She reinforced the effect by forward-paddling furiously with the right oar, forcing the raft to scrape up against the granite wall, hoping to shake Deke's grip. The raft dipped into a trough at the bottom of the tongue, then its bow shot up, propelling Deke back into the craft. He gripped the left canvas strap with his right hand and flung his left hand toward the right strap. He found it and held fast; he was now on his back in the bow, arms outstretched like Christ on the cross, eyes fixed on Gail. Water sloshed around his body.

** ** **

Tom exhaled as if he were on the river with them. "Fuck," he muttered at Gail's failed attempt to separate Deke from the raft. He bristled with pride, however—knowing that she was going to go down fighting, with or without her husband. It strengthened his own resolve to keep going.

** ** **

"*I'm watching you!*" Deke screamed at Gail as she swung the stern of the raft river right and pulled mightily to work them farther away from the cliff. Gail glanced over her shoulder to make sure Roarke was safe. Terry looked like he was going to throw up. That made her feel good. She straightened their course to sail down another chute. Ahead, she could see where the white water gave way to the deep green of the pool below, and to safe haven. She had one more piece of broken water to navigate. There was a chute of calmer water she could have chosen, but she pulled hard to position the raft further river right. Then she pushed hard, two handed, to accelerate their speed. The raft roller-coastered through the chop, *bumb, bump, bump* like a moguls skier, the bow snaking up and down, the flexible core of the raft lifting and falling as it slid over each small rock that made up this final section of the rapids. Deke glared at her all the while, his hands white with the exertion of holding fast. Gail realized she'd have to cut them off to loosen his contact with the raft and bounce him out. The raft took one last violent plunge at the foot of the rapids and squirted into deep, unbroken water.

She shipped her oars and looked at Roarke. "You okay, honey?" The boy offered a brave smile. Terry, who cradled him under one arm, was worse for wear; he was drenched and spooked. Deke relinquished his handholds and pushed himself into a seated position with his back nestled against the inside of the bow where the tubes came together. The sun burned overhead. Gail contemplated her next move even as the adrenaline receded in her body. Her arms and back ached.

"You cannot get me off this river soon enough," Terry said. "Takeout shouldn't be far now, right?"

Gail said nothing. Deke unfolded his map and peered at it. "Yeah, except we're not getting out at the takeout."

"What do you mean?" Terry asked his partner, bewildered. "I thought that was the whole idea. Grab a car and go."

"It was until I realized that maybe we ought to get off the river where people won't be expecting us to get off the river."

"Above the takeout?" Terry asked, confused.

Deke held up the map for Terry to see and pointed to their location a few miles above the takeout at Canyon Gorge. "It's like a goddamn conveyor belt. If anyone thought we were on the river, where do you think they'd wait for us?"

"What about the car?" Terry asked.

"Getting a car's less important than getting out unseen. Pull in up ahead," he told Gail.

The sudden change of plans alarmed Gail. "Takeout's only two miles ahead, Deke. Nothing you can't handle."

Deke pulled out his .22 and aimed it at Gail. "Pull over."

Gail aimed the stern of the raft river right and pulled for shore. They were one bend above Lieutenant Long's first line of defense. The raft beached itself in shallow water. Deke vaulted over the side and dragged the nose on shore. "Everybody out."

"Just leave us here, Deke," Gail said. "Take the raft when it's dark. Float down to the takeout or above it and walk out. Anybody can float this last section. It's nothing you can't handle."

"And then what?" he asked Gail. "Wait until you get picked up by the next boat? Or swim out? How much head start would that give us? You and Roarke get out and stand next to that cliff where I can see you. Terry, let's get the water out."

Gail and Roarke walked over to the base of the cliff. The two fugitives tilted the raft onto one gunwale until all the collected river water had drained out. "Grab the back end," Deke said. Deke grabbed the nose of the bow, Terry took the stern. Deke walked the raft into a stand of high grass and saplings where it couldn't be seen from the river.

"What do we do now, Deke?" Terry asked, impatiently. "What's the plan?"

"We wait," Deke told him.

27

Tom had moved slightly downriver for a better view of Gail's beached raft. It was hidden from sight, but he had watched Deke and Terry pull it away from the water's edge and into the stand of cottonwoods. Behind that, an overhang at the bottom of the cliff wall provided even more shelter from river travelers. As the afternoon wore on and full sunlight retreated from the river, Tom watched another half dozen rafts navigate Indian Gorge rapids and continue downstream.

By moving a few hundred yards downriver he could watch activity at the takeout. There were dozens of cars and trailers parked back from the ramp. A steady procession of trailers were backed into the water to engage and winch up the rafts that stayed inflated. Other rafts were pulled up on either side of the ramp to be deflated and packed out. Tom stopped to watch two fishermen work the bend just above the takeout, while two other guys set up camp. He saw no beached rafts, canoes, kayaks, or water masters, so it was unclear how they had gotten there.

** ** **

At dusk, the four members of the SWAT team gathered at the river's edge. They had diligently monitored the passing traffic; now, with fading light, visual contact was going to be more difficult. Radio communication in the canyon was nonexistent, but their orders were clear: maintain their position day and night until further apprised. Cumulous clouds bunched ever tighter in the portion of the sky they could see. Complete cloud cover would make visual monitoring next to impossible at night.

** ** **

Downstream, at the takeout, the last of the late-arriving traffic had come and gone. New cars and cars with trailers had shuttled into the parking lot all day long, transportation-to-be for rafters just putting in upriver. Thompson Littlebuck joined the lieutenant at the water's edge. Long was uncharacteristically edgy. "There's no other place they could climb out, right?"

"Not unless they're Spiderman," the ranger told him. "Maybe he's gonna try to slip out under the cover of darkness."

Bobby Long looked upriver. The air looked chalkier as the last reflected sunlight left the canyon floor. He stared overhead at the layer of clouds. He peered downriver, where the current narrowed and fell off toward the Gauntlet. He tried to get inside Deke's head. "What the fuck's he doing?"

** ** **

Deke slashed away at a cottonwood sapling with the camp hatchet and dropped the branches on the ground beside the raft. Terry sat under the overhang, sipping a beer, guarding Gail and Roarke. Deke returned with a final cut sapling and began lashing the cuttings on and around the raft. "I don't think you killed my friends," Gail said to Terry. "I think Deke did. It'll make a difference when they catch you . . . and they will. If you let Roarke and me go, I'll tell the court you helped me."

Terry looked at Gail. "You and Deke should be partners," he told her. "You think alike. I saw you and Deke together casting. There was something between you. I could tell. I can tell those things."

"You don't need us anymore is all I'm saying," Gail said. "Float to the takeout. There's no more rough water. Take our rental. It's a gray Toyota minivan. The key's in the gas cap. Take the car. I won't try to get out of here until daylight. I promise. That'll give you almost a day's head start. Get off the river, Terry, while you can. Things happen out here you can't control. I know. I spent ten years as a guide. I told Deke this and it's true, there are laws out here. Things happen you can never predict or control. The longer you stay on the river the surer it is that will happen."

Terry looked at Gail for the longest time, said nothing. Then he finished his beer. If nothing else, she was sure she had stirred some embers of second thoughts.

** ** **

Tom saw them launch the raft around midnight only because a gust of wind tore a hole in the cloud cover, and a beam of moonlight angled down onto the beach.

** ** **

The raft was camouflaged with cottonwood branches. Terry hoisted Roarke into the back, then stepped in beside him. Deke pushed the raft into deeper water. "Get in the bow," he told Gail. Gail climbed in. Deke waited until the moon vanished once more behind a dense quilt of clouds. Satisfied, he pushed off and took the oars mid-raft. He aimed the stern toward the far cliff wall. The current was smooth and even. Deke stroked until they bumped against the wall, then he pushed off to get an oar between the oar-lock and the wall and pointed the raft straight downstream. He removed his .22 from the back of his belt and aimed it at Gail. "Slide down," he told her. "Keep your head below the branches."

He turned to Terry. "You and Roarke, get your butts on the bottom of the raft." From water level, only Deke's head and shoulders were visible above the sapling camouflage. From shore, they could have been a fallen tree floating downriver.

** ** **

Three of the SWAT team members sat around a campfire they had built in a ring of river stones, eating packaged food. The fourth member sat on a rock by the river's edge, on lookout. He noticed a slight thickening in the water next to the cliff wall. It moved with the current, like a lump in the water. Curious, he clicked on his powerful flashlight. The flashlight beam hit the canyon wall first, in front of the raft, alarming Deke, giving him time to frantically ship his oars and slide his body onto the floor of the raft. The flashlight illuminated the leaves of the cottonwood branches poking out above the rounded black tubes of the Avon. Deke could see the light brighten the canyon wall just beyond the raft.

The SWAT team member saw nothing but a tree float by. Satisfied, he clicked off the beam and continued his vigil.

** ** **

From his vantage, Tom could make out the SWAT team's campfire on the far side of the river. He had seen the beam of light dance across the water's surface. The raft blended in well with the dark current. All he knew was that his wife and son were headed downriver . . . somewhere. He patted Maggie on the head and told her it was time to go. The moonless night offered limited visibility, but Tom had familiarized himself with the canyon rim and the terrain over the course of the day. He had marked out in his mind's eye the next station—one that would give him a perspective on the takeout.

** ** **

What he didn't see was the look in Deke's eyes after he elevated his head to peer through the cover of the cut branches after the flashlight beam went dark. It could have been just campers, harmlessly monitoring river traffic from the water's edge, but Deke's gut told him otherwise. He suspected his presence on the river was no longer a secret. But *where* on the river? That was an advantage he believed he still held.

** ** **

Bobby Long was talking to his horse in the parking lot when the camouflaged raft floated into the top of the run above Canyon Gorge takeout. The cloud cover held, and the trooper monitoring the river flow had walked back to the campfire to replenish his water bottle. Terry held Roarke against the bottom of the raft in the stern. Deke had the .22 pressed to Gail's head in the bottom of the front of the raft. Their legs were tangled up somewhere in the middle.

There was fear in Gail's eyes as she watched the distinctive, towering cliffs of Canyon Gorge pass overhead. "You're not getting off at the takeout."

Deke pressed his lips to Gail's ear. "No."

"There's nothing downriver but the Gauntlet."

"I know."

"We won't make it," Gail told him. "It's class VI white water . . . *suicide*."

"Well, it won't be for a lack of trying, will it? You've

already lost a husband to this river. It'd be a shame to lose his son."

** ** **

Tom MacDonald was every bit as worried as his wife. He crept along the rim of the canyon and watched the camouflaged raft float by the takeout and pass between the towering cliffs of Canyon Gorge—stone monoliths that looked like mythological pillars to a forbidden place. The raft pulled in to a scimitar-shaped beach carved out of the far side of the river—safe harbor above the cauldron of smashed water that represented the Gauntlet below.

Tom walked farther downstream and sat on a rock above the rumble of the river. He knew Deke was going to challenge the Gauntlet to make his escape. He assumed he'd wait till daylight to do it. Recalling the configuration of the river, how it made a horseshoe bend midway through the Gauntlet, he knew he would have to take the shortcut to the tail end and there make a stand—if there was anything to make a stand for. If Gail, somehow, survived the Gauntlet. It was a hypothetical based on a hypothetical, but at least he knew the *where*—which gave him a nub of hope.

While he was thinking these things, the cloud cover parted like curtains on the far side of the canyon, revealing translucent ribbons of coral- and cranberry-colored northern lights, the *aurora borealis*. They shimmered and swayed like the dresses of backup singers—shafts of gauzy, soft color. Tom was sure it was a sign that Mother Nature was telling him Gail was right: that there *was* a harmony in the wilderness, an unspoken order. He was not a religious person, but in that moment on the rim of that canyon, staring at something that took his breath away and stirred him in a most primitive way, he knew, even with so much uncertainty ahead, that there was a force for good in the world that was hard to explain but impossible to ignore— a version, perhaps, of Dr. King's moral arc. Faith. Hope. Help. Justice. Something inexplicable but true.

28

Trooper Page Noel couldn't sleep. He reprised the baying of the bloodhounds in his ears when he discovered Mary Walsh's red Ford Sedan and the poor woman's long-dead body. He had to admire Deke and Terry's misdirection at the railroad tracks, whether inadvertent or intended, that led to the lineup of traffic at the Sweet Grass border crossing. He was grateful for the tip that had narrowed the search to the River Wild, but there was much to be done, and too much still could go wrong. Because of that, he had a knot in his stomach when he climbed out of his Canyon Gorge takeout tent an hour before first light. He hoped the lieutenant might also be up; he wanted to talk. But Bobby Long was long gone. So were Marlene, his horse, and her trailer.

** ** **

The Lieutenant's attempts at sleep had been disturbed by the recurring image of the murdered Mary Walsh. He hadn't seen her in a few years, but she was a thread to a part of his life he cherished. He believed in the great continuum of life, that there were friends and lovers and family and events that stitched you back in time in a way that gave comfort to the journey. He loved her smile and her rough laugh, and the truth his wife required her to supply. He thought of her because he knew her, but her death rankled him beyond that. It was really a matter of unfairness. That a woman who had been voted Teacher of the Year year after year because she made her students in a hard-scrabble Deer Lodge elementary school believe in themselves even when the weight of failed romances made her give up on her own possibilities of sharing her life with someone else—that that same woman, Mary Walsh, had finally found a gentle man who loved her, only to be horrifically sabotaged by fellow human beings who valued life roughly on a par with cold beer—that made Bobby Long angry on top of sad. His first paying job came at age eleven, tossing bales of hay. It planted in him the belief that life was hard, but hard work would at least reward you with the wherewithal to afford a sufficiency of dignity to shepherd you through the tough times with moments of contentment, love, pride, adventure, friendship, memorable sex, and pan-seared rib-eyes. Though maybe not in that order.

Which explained why Detective Lieutenant Bobby Long of the Montana State Police was driving his vehicle and horse trailer down a neglected logging road in the dark five miles downstream of Canyon Gorge and a stretch of the River Wild called the Gauntlet. He was goddamned if William Deakens Patterson was going to stay at the chess board long enough to make the last move. He had described himself to Sergeant Noel as insurance, but in his old rodeo-ridin' heart he was sure it would come down to one last ride. Trooper Billy Heston sat shotgun beside the lieutenant, his head jiggling like a bobblehead doll on the rough road.

"Son, I'm going to tell you something so you don't make the mistake I made once. It's better not to lose sleep over things you should have done different." Long kept his eyes fixed on the road. "But first I'm going to give you something." He unsnapped a shirt pocket and handed Heston a laminated index card. Heston glanced at it. The edges were nicked with use. The once-clear laminate had yellowed over time. He struggled to read the typeface in the dark interior.

"It says you have the right to remain silent," the lieutenant told him. "Anything you say can and will be used against you. Etcetera." The young trooper offered it back.

"Keep it," the lieutenant told him. He patted his other shirt pocket. "I have another. Always have it on you." Long looked at him sternly. "*Always.*" Heston slid the card into his shirt pocket.

"Many years ago," the lieutenant continued, "I was at the tail end of my shift. It was early morning. Call came in over dispatch there was domestic trouble at a motel in this little speed-bump town of Wolf Creek. The motel owner met me in the dirt parking lot as I skidded in. She was wrapped in a bathrobe, she looked like hell. She held the robe around her with one hand and pointed at room 11 with her other. They were stand-alone units. The door to unit 11 was open, light spilled out. 'He hurt her bad,' she told me. 'Be careful.' I put in a call for backup, but the dispatcher said no units were available: ETA forty-five minutes. I realized I was on my own. So I drew my weapon and ghosted over to the unit. I tried to look in a small window, but it was too dirty to see through, so I crept up to the open door and just listened for a moment. All I could hear was Merle Haggard on the radio. He was singing "Kern River," and in the soft parts during the verse I could hear a girl sobbing. I was actually trying to decide if I should wait till the song was over to step in, but then I thought the song would give me cover so I stepped inside with my gun drawn. William Deakens Patterson was sitting on the bed, bare-chested, wearing blue jeans, drinking beer. There was blood on his chest and hands. There was a cooler on the floor beside him, filled with iced beer, empty beer bottles on the bedside bureau. There was a bunch of blood on the carpet. The door to the bathroom was open. Deke casually held out his hands when he saw me. 'Don't shoot,' he said. 'The bitch is in the bathroom. Yes, I know my Miranda rights, and no, I ain't talkin'.' I kept my weapon trained on him and edged over to the bathroom door. There was a naked girl in the tub, crying, sitting in a pool of her own blood as if the hotel were haunted and blood instead of water came out of the faucet."

Long glanced at Billy Heston in the dark cab. "Mo Udall once said about his hometown in Utah, it wasn't the end of the world, but you could see the end of the world from there. That's where I was." He returned his eyes to the road. The horse trailer brushed back overhanging branches. "In a place not too much more civilized than this. On my own. Without backup. I figured I had a girl bleeding out. I had a verbal Miranda, so I cuffed Deke and put him in the back of my car. Then I attended to the girl and called an ambulance. At that point, I was probably thinking more about what *could go wrong* than *what I was doing right*. I drove the thirty-odd miles to Helena. I clicked on the video camera and sound recorder just in case. The son of a bitch talked almost the whole way. The violence must have been some kind of rush. He confessed to cuttin' her with his knife. Said she was trash. Young pussy, which he said he liked, but trash. Disposable. He had picked her up in a bar. She told him she'd run away from home, so he knew he could do what he wanted. Have sex. Get drunk. Cut her up for fun. He didn't hurt her until she said she didn't like Hagg, or any country music. She got sick of listening to it in her parents' home. So he cut her. Said he'd keep cutting her until she said she liked it. I took him to Helena County jail and booked his sorry ass. I booked his knife into evidence. I gave them a thumb drive of the conversation and tape from my car and they burned a disk or something—you know what that shit is—and they sealed the confession in an envelope with the police report number.

"As the hearing for the trial date approached, I got a call from the DA's office. They said the girl had disappeared. They had lost their only witness. The assistant DA said they couldn't find a written waiver for Deke's confession in the file, and that's all we had left—his confession. I told them he had verbally waived his Miranda rights, and they said okay, they'd check the tape, but there wasn't one there, either. They told me we had a problem. At the hearing the day before the trial, we're all in court and the defense files a motion to suppress and the judge says to prosecution, 'People would you like to be heard?' And my guy looks at me with a sick look—I was seated in the public section—and there's nothing he can say because I fucked up and didn't get a waiver on paper or tape, because I thought I had one, and I was a little tired and running on adrenaline, and because Deke had talked on tape for half an hour about how he had hurt that girl. And then the judge says, 'I'm going to grant the motion.' And he ordered the case dismissed and the defendant to be released forthwith . . . *forthwith!*

"It was the second-worst day of my life, after my wife dying. The bailiff uncuffed Deke, and he walked out a free man, but not before stopping in front of me sitting there in that courtroom, fuming. He could tell I was about to burst. He leaned close, gave me a shit-eating grin, and said, 'You have the right to remain silent.'"

They skidded around a bend at probably too much speed; a deadfall pine blocked the road. Long, preoccupied with his story and driving on autopilot, swore violently as he jammed his foot against the brake pedal. The tires of his pickup locked. He could hear the weight of Marlene's chest slam into the front of her trailer. The horse whinnied. The truck, propelled by the added weight of the trailer, skidded across the dirt road, coming to a stop inches from contact. "Jesus fucking Christ," Long pronounced. His first concern was Marlene. He pulled on the hand brake and hopped out of the truck. He put his hand through the opening near the front of the trailer. He patted the horse. "You okay, girl? My fault. End of the road for you."

Five minutes later the lieutenant was tightening Marlene's saddle as Billy Heston looked on. Satisfied, Bobby Long hooked a cowboy boot in the stirrup and hoisted himself atop his horse.

"You know him better than anyone, Lieutenant," Heston said, a little embarrassed to be lecturing his boss, though his intentions were born of the heart, not the head.

"Deke doesn't make much distinction between living and dying."

The lieutenant checked the magazine of his lever-action Winchester rifle and slid it back into his saddle holster. "If he's alive when I get to him, he's gonna wish he weren't. C'mon, girl!"

He prodded Marlene to circle around the root mass of the tree. It was still dark, but a tinge of pinkness from the direction of the river indicated dawn was on deck. Heston watched the lieutenant steer Marlene back onto the dirt road on the far side of the tree. He squeezed her with his knees, made a *clicking* sound, and off she went on a trot.

** ** **

Having taken the short leg between the prongs of the river's giant horseshoe, Tom and Maggie found themselves standing at first light on a forty-foot cliff above a deep pool downstream of the Gauntlet. A tributary carved a steep, obstructing gorge below where they stood, preventing any further progress by land. A sheer cliff faced them on the far side. Below the pool on the main river, there was a section of mild rapids, and below that the river evened out into slow, froggy water with rolling meadows on either side. This was the final stretch, where the river—exhausted by its wild ride through the Gauntlet—took a lazy breath before dumping into the Missouri River.

Tom took in the jump once more: higher than was comfortable but survivable. Man and dog backed up for a running start. They launched themselves almost at the same time, sailed through the air for a few harrowing seconds, and plunged into the pool several yards apart. Tom bobbed to the surface to find Maggie already dog paddling in circles looking for him. Tom back-paddled to slow their speed as the tail-out of the pool began to sweep them ever faster into the start of the rapids. Man and dog angled close together. Tom draped an arm over the retriever's back. "Okay, Mags . . . show me your stuff."

Whoosh . . . they were swept into the first white water. Tom remembered to swing his feet downstream to protect himself from rocks. Maggie flailed with her forepaws to keep her head above water as they glided down a first spill and into a chute. A knifelike rock parted the current dead ahead. Tom pulled with his right arm to steer them to the right of the rock. He sailed by and was plunged into a tumble of white froth. When he made it back to the surface, the current rushed him toward a fallen log, angling out of the riverbank. He gulped a fresh breath and ducked below the surface to avoid being knocked out. He lost his grip on Maggie in the maneuver, and when he popped up downstream of the log he was separated from the dog. He could see her flailing away in the churn of a rapids that stretched from bank to bank, but he couldn't reach her. He was too busy eying the deeper, calmer water now only forty feet away. Safe harbor.

Maggie was first to be propelled over the mossy ledge and into the deeper water. She popped up safely ten feet downstream and immediately began paddling in circles, barking, looking for Tom.

Tom sailed over the ledge and plunged into the pool below. He hit the uneven river bottom with considerable force—jamming one foot between rocks. The strength of the current pushed him forward, wedging the foot even tighter between the rocks. Tom looked down in panic. His foot was lodged in a way that made it almost impossible to free up without moving upstream against the powerful current. He stroked with all his might, but he couldn't pull free. Maggie circled just downriver, looking for him; Tom could see her paws pushing against the water. He looked down once more: he was running out of air. Desperate, he planted his free foot on the rock beside the lodged foot for better leverage. He pushed as hard as he could, simultaneously wrenching his body. His trapped foot popped free, minus ear-sized flaps of skin on either side of his ankle. The clear water turned crimson. The pain was searing. Tom let out a scream that was muffled by the din of the rapids and turned into a rush of bubbles. The bubbles flew upward, toward Maggie and the blue beyond.

** ** **

Two miles above Indian Gorge takeout, two of Long's
SWAT team members stood thigh deep in the river, holding fly rods, peering upstream for any glimpse of boat
traffic. The third team member stood below them, not far
from their tent, wearing shorts and flip-flops. His sniper's
rifle was angled against the back of the cottonwood towering beside him, out of sight from any river traffic.

At the takeout itself, Trooper Noel sat on the back of a
boat trailer parked beside the boat ramp. The van marked
Bear Canyon Anglers was visible in the line of parked cars.
Two other troopers wearing outdoor recreational gear
sipped coffee nearby. Just upstream of the takeout, another
trooper sat in a collapsible camp chair wedged into the
sand at the water's edge. He wore shorts and a fishing shirt.
Binoculars were slung around his neck. On the sand beside
him, the handle of his police revolver poked out of a rum-
pled beach towel. From his vantage, he could see a hundred yards upstream.

** ** **

If they had known to look downstream toward the Gauntlet and had the ability to see through a wall of granite, they
would have seen Roarke and Gail sitting on the scrap of
beach at the foot of cliffs that elsewhere rose up sheer from
the river. Terry sat on the edge of the raft, nervously watching Deke, who stood at the far end of the beach, peering
downstream at a place where the lead edge of the River
Wild seemed to just fall away.

Gail held Roarke's face in her hands. "We have a shot at this, honey, and I think someone's looking out for us, but if you end up in the water, try to keep your feet angled downstream, right? . . . So you hit any rocks feet first. You're not going to believe how fast the current is. Luckily, you're a great swimmer, so that's going to help if you get separated from the raft."

"What about you, Mom?"

"Well, I'm going to try to keep the raft afloat and us in it, but you always need a Plan B in life, right?" She glanced at Deke and Terry. "These guys can't swim, which is good if we end up in the river. Here's the other thing. The old logging road is on this side of the river. The take-out side. So if and when, or when and if we . . . or you, get to the bottom of the Gauntlet—and you'll know that because it's really froggy and slow—get out to river right and head away from the river. You'll hit the road at some point. Take a right, upstream, and that'll hit the road to the takeout where there are always people."

"Gail!" Deke's voice pierced the dull rumble of the river. Gail looked at Deke, who had returned to the raft and was signaling it was time to go.

"I'm scared," Roarke said, softly.

Gail kissed him. "Me, too. But you know what? We're going to get through this somehow—'cause my gut says so—and we're going to meet up with Dad and Maggie and oh boy, are you going to have the best story to tell your class when your teacher asks everyone what they did this summer. You'll probably win an award."

Roarke blinked back tears.

"You know what else?" Gail told him. "You're the best kid I ever had. And I'm not even kidding. Not even close."

** ** **

Minutes later, Gail was seated at the oars of the raft—now shorn of its branch camouflage. She watched Deke tie Roarke's feet to a D ring near the bottom of the raft. Her face tightened. "He's got no chance if we flip, Deke."

"Which makes him even with me and gives you all the more incentive to keep the boat afloat, doesn't it? Besides, Roarke told me you've done this before."

"I was twenty years younger. And I rowed every day."

"Let's hope it's just like riding a bike, then. You get us through the Gauntlet, to that road out, and I'll let you go. How's that? Deal?"

Deke spotted the camp hatchet in a mesh net inadvertently packed within reach of Gail. He leaned over and retrieved the hatchet. "Don't want to leave any sharp objects within reach of children," and with a look, he said, "or their *parents*." He slipped the hatchet into a storage net near his bow position.

Terry climbed in beside Roarke and lowered himself into the bottom of the raft. Deke edged the bow of the raft off the beach. He looked downstream. He couldn't see the Gauntlet, but he could hear the rumble it made. "Drivers start your engines," he said, stepping into the bow of the raft as he pushed them gently free of shore. "Drive safely, now. We have children on board."

"Deke," Gail said. She leaned forward and gestured for him to come closer. There was a hardness in her eyes that was almost unnatural. She placed her lips by his ear. "Do you know what the Ma Morgan Society is?"

"Tell me."

"It's a secret society of mothers. I'm a member. There's only one rule. Do you know what that rule is?"

"No."

"If you hurt my family, *I will kill you.*"

She sat back and pulled hard on the oars, jerking Deke off his feet and onto the bottom of the raft. She rowed into the center of the current before straightening out the raft's trajectory. She turned to Roarke and pulled him against her body. "I love you," she told him. "Buckle up. Hang on."

The river narrowed at the tail end of the pool as it bent river left. Forced in by the guarding pillars, the current picked up speed, moving the raft at a faster clip. Gail braced herself with her oars to stand and assess and slowly back-oar. The start of the Gauntlet rushed into view—a bristle of white water, bank to bank. Gail stared downriver, imagining her run. She flew back in time to the only time she had ever taken in this view. Adrenaline surged in her body as it had twenty years earlier. Fear was matched by gumption. Back then she had soloed the run. There was only one passenger she cared about now, and it wasn't even her. *Though if Tom was dead* it would be her job alone to shepherd Roarke to a place where he was strong enough to manage all of life's currents on his own. She sat down, empowered. She made one last course correction before the current swept them into the unbroken water and plunged the raft down a first chute.

The raft bounced easily over the first mogul field of rapids, snaking its way across the top of the churn, the fairly even weight distribution of bow, midraft, and stern gluing the raft's rubber bottom to the water's surface. Deke gripped the canvas lifting straps on either side of the bow. He practically pressed himself against the bottom. The raft hit a sizable curl-back, and the nose shot up. Gail drove both oars forward to counterbalance the backward thrust and help force the nose back down. It slapped down, taking aboard a spray of water that soaked everyone. Deke allowed himself to peek over the top of the bow. For a good hundred yards, there was nothing but acres of angry, churning water. Beyond that, the river began its major horseshoe bend to the left—a stretch where centrifugal force smashed half the current against the outer cliff.

Gail worked her oars the way a mogul skier used her poles, little plants here and there to keep the momentum forward and hold the raft to its line. It took concentration and strength. When Deke's body angled too far in one direction, Gail shouted at him to "Center up!" A dangerous rock rose up dead ahead, causing the river to cleave around it. Gail furiously dug in with her left oar to aim her butt river right. One, two powerful strokes to get the stern off its line, then two-handed strokes to try to cut through the chop and avoid a collision. She grunted with the exertion, pressed her feet hard against the bottom of the raft for better leverage. She took two more strokes, then scrambled to swivel the bow once more directly downstream. The raft just cleared the rock, brushing against it. The current rushed them toward the bend. Like a downhill skier,

Gail knew she had to take as much of an inside line as she could—not for speed but for safety. She swung the butt violently the other way, river left, to try to get her closer to the inside line that would keep the current from smashing her up against the outer wall.

Roarke's eyes widened with alarm as the raft hurtled toward the midway point of the Gauntlet—the hairpin turn left. Ahead, where the force of the current was forced through a narrows that halved the width of the river, the noise was deafening. Terry was ashen.

"Mom!" Roarke hollered. He was afraid.

Gail yelled at him over her shoulder: "We're okay. Get down. Hang on!"

All of a sudden, Gail caught a crab with her left oar. It was partly because the raft abruptly dipped down as she dug in with her oar. The water held the blade and wouldn't let go. The force of the current pushed the raft forward and punched the oar handle out of Gail's left hand. The raft swung crazily broadside in the chop. Gail jerked her right oar out of the water as she lunged to grab her other oar before it slipped through the oarlock and overboard. Water poured over the right gunwale as the raft tried to manage the chop sideways. Imbalanced, the raft hit the next rock broadside. Gail leaped to the upstream rail to keep it from flipping. The raft folded dangerously in the midsection then sprung loose around the rock so that they were now turned stern-first downriver. Gail fumbled to return both oars to their oarlocks. Water sloshed around her feet, further destabilizing their ride. The cliffs narrowed dangerously, speeding up the current. All she could hear was the rumble around the corner, where the Gauntlet underwent a massive churn to alter course. It would be almost impossible to survive bow first. Sideways, they were dead.

Gail sunk back into her seat, yanked her left oar onboard and grabbed the right oar two-handed to dig into the current and swing them around. She grunted and swore. She got red in the face. She rose up in a crouch and pushed for all she was worth. Her thighs screamed at her. Reluctantly, the bow edged downstream. When she had them aligned north and south, Gail slid the other oar back into action. She still had to get them closer to the inside line to survive the plunge. She aimed her butt river left and inched the raft closer to the cliff. The current swept them into the turn, ready or not. The river seemed to stampede itself toward the outer wall. There were whitecaps the size of ocean waves between her and the far cliff. Where the current collided with the wall, there was deadly chaos. The raft was practically shaking from all the torque on it. The river wanted to hurl it against its outer cliff, dooming it. Gail pulled two-oared in short, powerful, choppy strokes, all the time keeping her butt river left to hug the inner wall. Her arms throbbed with fatigue, felt like rubber. She persisted out of fear.

What Deke saw next made him piss in his pants. Literally. As they swung around the pivot point of the inner cliff and started to straighten out, the bottom of the river fell out. This was the legendary Niagara Falls of the Gauntlet, more commonly known to guides and river dogs as "the drowning field." The noise was deafening. Deke glanced back at Gail. What she saw in his face—for the first time—

was a terror brought on by a complete loss of control. Behind her, Terry puked partly from fear, partly because he had swallowed so much water. Roarke reached forward and wrapped his arms around Gail's waist. The lip of the waterfall raced at them. For a moment, when she looked straight ahead, all Gail could see was air and sky.

The waterfall stretched from bank to bank; there was no intermediate trail down. The final obstacle, if you survived the plunge, was the Sphinx—a monolith right in the middle of the river that cleaved the boiling current left and right, leading to deeper, smoother water downriver and safe harbor. If you hit the Sphinx, the hydraulics guaranteed you were dead. It was as treacherous and merciless as the desert icon for which it was named.

Gail centered herself and made a final adjustment so that the raft could take the falls properly aligned—north and south. The river fell away, and they were suddenly airborne. Only the underside of the stern of the raft maintained contact with the river. Gail leaned back like a bronc buster to keep the raft from nosediving and flipping forward when it hit. She angled the oars back as well, ready to engage the river on contact and with a mighty back-paddle help counter the raft's forward momentum. Terry and Deke were screaming, but the roar of the river buried their voices. The bow pierced the water first like a pelican dive-bombing for fish. There was enough weight in the back half of the raft to allow the rubber nose of the Avon to pop up moments later, gouging water. A curtain of water poured over the sides, and for a moment the raft seemed to stick in place, held by powerful up-current. Gail knew she had to break out or be swamped. She shipped her left oar and grabbed the right two-handed. She rose up like a gondolier and back-oared two-handed. She had to generate enough speed to break out of the eddy. The waterfall poured down upon her and Roarke and Terry. Deke clung to the bow. Gail got the boat spinning, slowly at first, then faster and faster with each stroke, finally generating enough speed to break free. The raft caught in the downstream surge once more and rushed ahead, toward the Sphinx. Gail sunk back into her seat and returned the shipped oar to action. She back-paddled with the remaining strength she had to slow their speed and give her a chance of maneuvering the raft left or right. Her strength was ebbing. She had to make her play, or they'd be carried into the Sphinx. She jammed her left oar into the current and back-paddled with her right. She shouted and grunted and pleaded and growled. Suddenly, the stern swung river left, giving her just enough of a purchase on the current to make her move out of the suicidal current that targeted the Sphinx. She sunk back into her seat and rowed, pretending she was back on the Charles River for the last gasp to and through the Longfellow Bridge. She pulled until the Sphinx loomed almost overhead, then she stabbed her left oar into the water to swing the bow downstream.

The raft straightened out just as the current washed it up against the flank of the Sphinx. The right side rode up slightly against the rock, but the force of the current pushed the nose downriver and into the final chute that emptied into the still water that marked the end of the Gauntlet. The raft slipped through the final, accelerated current and

over a last turbulence before being squirted into the head
of the long, deep, green pool below.

Gail released the oars and collapsed from the exertion
into the six inches of water in the bottom of the raft. She
lay still, panting, like an Olympic cross-country skier at the
end of a final sprint. The rumble of the waterfalls receded.
After a moment, Deke's eyes peered up over the bow. At
the back of the raft, Roarke and Terry pulled themselves
up onto the inflated gunwales. They looked like survivors
of a tornado, lifting the cover of a root cellar to see what
remained of their world.

29

The river below the Sphinx was as peaceful and tranquil as it was wild above. The cliffs faded away to rolling hills. The river straightened and deepened. There were any number of overhanging cottonwoods, some of which sported thick ropes knotted at the bottom for kids to unleash summertime cannonballs and belly flops.

Deke was studying the soaked river map.

"About a mile to the logging road," Gail told him. "Leave us here. You'll be off the river soon. We'll walk out."

Deke refolded the map. "There's been a change of plans."

Gail froze. "There's no one coming after us, Deke. No one's on the river down here but us."

"It's not who's coming after you that worries me. The problem is, once you get out, the folks who have been chasing us will know they still need to chase us. But if you're not there to tell them, and they find the raft overturned and they find your body and Roarke's—*drowned*—they're going to have to believe we didn't make it either . . . the Gauntlet being the Gauntlet." He smiled. "*What was she thinking taking a child down the Gauntlet*? Dead *and* irresponsible!" He shrugged.

"We don't need to do any more killing, Deke," Terry said.

"How about some raping first? That's what you want, lover-boy, isn't it? *But first some bungi-bungi.* I told you you could do what you wanted once she got us through the Gauntlet."

"You told me we had a deal," Gail said, her voice raw with anger and betrayal. "I did what I said I'd do—I got you down this beautiful and wild river alive . . . now keep your end of the fucking bargain!"

"You know what hurts me most?" Deke replied, oozing a sincerity that had comingled with sarcasm for so long as to become indecipherable. "More than me giving you my word, then not living up to it? To think of you being the calf that makes it through the winter and dies in the spring. A farmer's nightmare. I know because my daddy was a farmer. At least he was until he beat me with a belt one day, as he did almost every day, and I put a pitch fork through his neck that night after he passed out on the kitchen floor. I know he would have felt the same."

Gail stopped slow-paddling and shipped the oars. It was all she knew to do to buy more time. She turned to Roarke and touched his wet hair. She had no words, no strength. He was crying even though he was attempting to put on a brave face for his mother. The raft glided beneath an overhanging tree. Gail looked up to where the branch thickened in an unnatural way. She looked down, then she looked up again. Tom angled his face into view. He had pressed his body to the limb in almost perfect camouflage. He put a "shush" finger to his lips, then silently retreated behind the limb to blend in once more as the raft drifted past.

Gail sat straight up. Her heart sang. Her body surged with adrenaline. Her mind raced, even though there was only one topic on the agenda: how to convene a meeting of the Ma Morgan Society.

** ** **

A bare-chested Tom hobbled downriver, propelled by a mix of desperation and adrenaline. His cut foot was wrapped with strips torn from his shirt. His exposed back was a massive, open, scabbed sore. His hair was a tangle. His one-time threat to Gail that the wilderness might bring out his inner beast had come true.

His destination was close by, where a giant cotton-wood had sunk its roots on the riverbank and lived for a hundred years or more. A limb from the tree angled out over the river. One kid's rope was knotted around the far end of the limb, some twenty feet over the water. The rope was drawn back and held in the crotch of a sapling. A second rope, affixed by Tom to the limb a couple yards closer to shore, was tied to a tree stump the size of a beer keg. The stump rested atop a rock nestled between giant roots.

Tom sunk down beside the tree trunk, picked up a lance he had fashioned from a branch, and took a few more strokes with his pocket knife on the point of the weapon. The branch was green and strong. Where he had carved away the bark to form the point, the wood gleamed white. Tom set the lance atop the rock. He lifted a club he had cut from a tree stump and tested its heft, two handed. It was like an Irish shillelagh, except the head was the size of a grapefruit, not a baseball. Tom took a swing with the club. It felt strong, potentially lethal. He placed the club on the rock beside the spear. Then he climbed up onto the rock and hoisted the stump in two hands. He backed up a step to put more tension on the rope. He peered upriver through the canopy of cottonwood leaves and river's edge brush. He waited.

** ** **

On board the raft, Gail took stock of everyone's positioning. She back-oared slowly, to gain time as she glanced around for potential weapons or booby traps she could fashion to aid Tom's ambush—whenever, and from wherever it would come. The oars, she knew, she could wield as needed. An actual lethal weapon—her hatchet—was a lunge away, visible in the mesh net of her backpack at Deke's feet in the bow. The anchor line was scattered at her feet. She looked back and glimpsed the anchor itself—a ten-pound pyramid of lead, jam-cleated in place, dangling off the stern. She smiled at Roarke, seated side by side with Terry. Knowing any attack would come from shore, she discretely eyed the angled limb of the giant cottonwood and adjusted their course so the raft would float beneath it. In the bow, Deke removed the .22 from the plastic trash liner he had wrapped it in. He opened the chamber and slid in six bullets. He nonchalantly glanced at Gail. He closed the chamber, rewrapped the revolver in the trash liner, and shoved it in his belt above his butt. Then he sat upright, closed his eyes, and let the sun warm him.

Tom glimpsed the raft through the thicket of cotton-wood leaves and branches and watched it to gauge its speed. He counted silently in his head. When the nose of the raft edged into view, just upriver of the overhanging limb, Tom drew a breath, took in Deke's head above the log he held, led him just a little given the current, and released the log. It swung out from the shadows of the bank and slammed into Deke's shoulder and head, knocking him out of the raft.

Terry watched it unfold before him. Almost in slow motion, he leaped to his feet. Gail was ready with the oars. She back-paddled with one and fore-paddled with the other—jerking the raft—knocking Terry, ass over tea kettle, off his feet. Gail snatched the loose end of anchor line and took two quick wraps around Terry's flailing ankles. She secured the loops with a half hitch, then jerked the line out of the jam-clete, releasing the anchor. Under the cottonwood boughs, Tom tossed the shillelagh onto the beach. He uncinched the second rope and stuck the knot between his legs. He grabbed the lance in his right hand, and held the rope with his left. He gauged the speed of the raft once more, then stepped off the rock. The tree limb groaned with his weight. Tom held the lance in his right hand, like a medieval jouster. The shaft of the weapon was wedged between his arm and body. Tom sailed through the air.

Terry staggered to his feet just as the anchor hit bottom and took hold. Propelled by the current, the raft continued its forward motion until the slack in the anchor line ran out, stopping the raft abruptly, jerking Terry off his feet once more. The raft's altered trajectory threw Tom's targeting out of sync. Instead of an intended deadly collision with Terry, he landed clumsily in the now stationary bow of the raft, crashing into Gail, who was fumbling for her hatchet. Roarke yelped involuntarily when he saw his father, his face splashed with joy. "*Dad!*" Tom got to his feet first and raised his spear, two handed overhead. Wild eyed, he lunged at Terry, who partially evaded the blow as he scrambled onto the side of the raft. The crude lance pierced his upper torso and emerged just under his right shoulder blade. He thrashed wildly to get out of the raft, but his lassooed foot was held tight by the rope and the jam-cleat. Gail cleved the rope with one swing of the hatchet, sending a skewered Terry overboard.

Roarke, facing downstream, saw Deke surface and begin to dog paddle groggily for shore. "Deke's getting away," the boy hollered, pointing.

"What about Terry?" Tom asked Gail.

"He can't swim," she said.

Tom vaulted over the bow of the raft and splashed toward his shillelagh on the bank. He was a man possessed. He grabbed the weapon and turned to finish off Deke, who was nearing the bank. The log had opened a gash over his left temple. Blood streamed down his face.

Terry, in deeper water and screaming in agony, turned over and over—thrashing grotesquely. First one end of the lance poked the surface, then the other. Then he was still. The body slipped below the green, even current. There was a slight rippling—reflecting one last twitch or reflex below the surface—then the water was still. Only Terry's blood was visible, floating downstream in an ever-expanding red stain. Gail leaped back into her rower's seat and stroked for all she was worth to help Tom.

Gagging and gasping, the nonswimming Deke finally touched bottom and struggled for dry land. Ten yards away Tom hobbled toward him. Maggie joined the fray, barking like crazy from the bank, frantically scrambling upstream and down, unsure where to be or go.

"Mom, it's Mags!" Roarke screeched in a voice as shrill as it was joyful.

Deke, in chest-deep water, fumbled for his .22 stuck in his belt. Tom, frantic to reach him before he could reach the gun, splashed toward the fugitive, alternately staggering, sinking to his knees, regaining his footing on the uneven bottom. Deke finally unwrapped the revolver and swung it on Tom. Tom froze, a body-length away, gripping the shillelagh in both hands. He fought to catch his breath, to quell his disappointment. Deke held the gun upright, then twisted it sideways, gangster-style. He smiled malevolently—in control once more. He and Tom just stared at each other for the longest moment. Deke was visibly baffled—imagining himself to be looking at a ghost.

"Goddamnit, Tom. Do I gotta kill you *again*?"

Gail took one last mighty stroke, propelling the raft faster than the current, closing the distance between her and Deke. She shipped her oars and picked up the hatchet. Deke cocked the gun and sighted Tom at the end of the short barrel.

"You gotta stay dead this time," he said. His finger closed on the trigger.

Gail—channeling Ma Morgan—reared back and let the hatchet fly. Hatchet throwing wasn't on her list of outdoor skills, but the distance was short and the goal was more diversionary than deadly. The hatchet spun through the air. . . handle over blade and thudded into Deke's rib cage. It didn't stick, but its impact was enough to knock him off balance. He staggered awkwardly, lowering both arms into the water to help him regain his footing. He didn't see Tom bring the shillelagh down on his head, knocking him out cold. Tom stood over the bobbing body, his club raised in case another blow was needed. There was a look in his eye as fierce as the River Wild.

"You want a piece of me?" he rasped through swollen lips. Tom swayed unsteadily, momentarily losing his footing. He lowered his face closer to Deke. "I can't hear you," he whispered. "*You want a piece of me?!*" He closed his eyes; he was about to pass out. He straightened up and took a deep breath. He began to drag Deke ashore by his hair.

Maggie, looking down from the bank, suddenly stopped wagging a happy tail. Her fur stood on end. She lowered her head and growled at Tom. Her lips were curled, her fangs bared. "It's okay, Mag, it's me," Tom said, soothingly.

Maggie snarled in an evil, foreboding way, as if she were rabid. Her growls grew louder and louder as Tom approached the bank. Terry surged out of the river behind Tom, holding a rock over his head. The lance stuck out of him, front and back; blood flowed freely from both wounds. His face was grotesquely twisted.

Gail screamed from the raft, "*Tom . . . behind you!*"

Tom released Deke and whirled. As Terry started to bring the rock down, a shot echoed across the water. A bullet slammed into Terry's chest, staggering the big man. He held the rock in both hands, but his eyes were glazed with surprise. He looked past Tom, toward the riverbank. Detective Lieutenant Bobby Long, gripping the saddle of his horse Marlene with his knees, cranked the lever action on his Winchester and fired again. The second round shattered Terry's forearm, driving him backwards, forcing him to drop the rock. The lieutenant cranked the lever once more. He urged his horse forward with his knees. Marlene slow-stepped to the edge of the river. Long trained his rifle on Terry in case another shot was needed. Terry lurched like a drunk, trying to find his footing on the uneven river bottom. He peered at the state trooper with the most quizzical expression. *How did it come to this?* Then he keeled over.

30

The ear-piercing *rhaaaaaannnnnng* of a chainsaw could be heard all the way down to the water's edge. In this case, it was a welcome intrusion. Trooper Heston steadied the saw through the last slice of the toppled pine blocking the logging road. With the help of a dozen other state troopers the obstruction was cleared. It's fair to say there were more vehicles backed up on that logging road than had been on it in the past five years: ten Montana State Police vehicles, two wilderness Search and Rescue Emergency vehicles, the local coroner, two pool press vehicles, and three local TV vehicles from station outlets in Great Falls and Helena.

** ** **

Within an hour, the logging road—where it dead-ended at the river's edge—looked like a makeshift takeout location, with vehicles parked everywhere. Marlene had been returned to her trailer. Trooper Noel watched Terry's stretcher get loaded into one ambulance. Deke was next. An oxygen mask covered his face. His wrists were handcuffed to a stretcher carried by four troopers. Lieutenant Long stopped the men before they slid the prisoner into the back of a second ambulance. He leaned over Deke and just looked at him for the longest time. Then he pulled a laminated card out of his shirt pocket and looked deliberately at the copy. If he had been a religious man, he might have sensed an exorcism of demons, fleeing his body. When he finally spoke, he said to Deke, "You have the right to remain silent. Anything you say can and will be used against you."

∗∗ ∗∗ ∗∗

Gail spread out the lieutenant's map of the river on the hood of a trooper's cruiser. Lieutenant Long, Sergeant Noel, and Ranger Thompson Littlebuck leaned in. Gail pointed out the Ten Mile Campsite where they were supposed to meet Jim and Peter and had encountered Deke and Terry instead. It was ten miles below the put-in at Hot Springs. "We were going to meet there because it was an easy float for Jim and Peter and a fishy place to stop. The plan was they'd spend a day getting there, then have a whole day to wade fish, waiting for us. I didn't give it too much thought when Deke and Terry told us the story about Jim cutting himself and the two of them deciding to row out. It just seemed like bad luck. The raft and the camp gear were rented, so it wasn't as if Deke and Terry had pretended the gear was their own gear. Mostly, I was just worried for our friends. I have to say Tom was suspicious from the start." A sudden sadness welled up within her. "I had been telling them for years how special this river was. . . . This was the first time we were able to put the trip together."

The lieutenant put a comforting hand on her shoulder. "They're not dead until we find the bodies. Maybe they just knocked them out and tied them up."

Gail looked haunted. "Deke showed us Jim's credit card after they took us hostage . . . said it was a terrible thing to expire before your credit card."

"You have to remember Deke's a pathological liar. Is there an easy way into that campsite by land?" the lieutenant asked Littlebuck.

"It's pretty rugged. I think jet boating in from Hot Springs would get you there quicker."

"Let's redeploy the SWAT team," Long told Trooper Noel. "Comb the site. Maybe get some dogs in."

The mention of dogs triggered a memory for Gail. "Just before we left the site that morning," she said, "Maggie got into something on the hill behind where we camped. She was barking like crazy. It wasn't like her. Tom went to get her, and now that I think about it, Deke hustled after him . . . supposedly to help. I don't know. Maybe it was nothing . . ."

Trooper Noel moved off to get on his walkie-talkie.

"I'm staying until we find Jim and Peter," Gail said. She brushed away tears. "But what do I tell their wives, Lieutenant? They don't know anything's wrong."

Bobby Long had endured more than his share of mayhem and misery. As a kid he had viewed life as mostly fun. Now, a long way downstream, he had come to accept the opposite: that life was mostly hard, and fun was the exception. Once you figured that out, it put disappointment in perspective. "Tell them the truth," the lieutenant told Gail.

"Their husbands are missing on the river, and there's the possibility of foul play. We're dispatching men to the site where they were last seen."

** ** **

Photographers took pictures of the raft, and of Tom and Gail and Roarke and Bobby Long, each involved with different activities. Even Maggie got her own close-up. The lieutenant told a circle of reporters—print and online media—that two other people, friends of the MacDonalds', were missing. Their names were being withheld until next of kin could be notified. Search and rescue efforts were commencing even as they spoke. "We will continue to update you on those efforts."

When asked about the manhunt and final ambush, the lieutenant said, "It was mostly good police work, a little luck . . . and maybe a voice in my head. Tell you what, though, what those folks endured to get off this river, to survive . . . *her* getting them down the Gauntlet alive at her age . . . *the Gauntlet!* I've had the best white water guys in the West, half her age, tell me they'd rather take their chances with a black mamba bite than tackle that piece of hell. *Him* escaping and never giving up . . . a city guy, basically, with no experience in the wilderness, with no hope

. . . climbing cliffs, swimming rivers, somehow figuring a way to save his wife from those two . . . that's the story. I was insurance and happy to provide it. But *their* story . . . that's the one you want."

Roarke was telling a piece of it at the river's edge to a cameraman and female reporter. He had one arm slung over Maggie. "I wasn't scared most of the time because Mom, you know, used to guide on this river. She knows what she's doing. And Pop . . . " Roarke caught a glimpse of his father having his back and ankle attended to by medical personnel as Gail supervised, "he really kicked some butt." He was bursting with pride.

"Pretty good for a guy from Brookline Village."

One of the medical personnel asked Tom if he wanted to be carried out on a stretcher. Tom told him crutches would do. The team measured, altered, and provided a set. "Can you give me a few minutes?" Tom said somberly. He and Gail made their way to the water's edge, away from the chaos.

For the longest time they just stared at the river. Then Tom said, "You know that what happened here changes us, forever." Gail half-smiled acknowledgment. "Of all the things we've ever done, this resets everything. Nothing will ever be the same."

Relief and sadness rushed through Gail like runoff, overwhelming any ability to contain or explain its flow in a meaningful way. "How is it," she wondered, "you can live for so long, and all of a sudden your life gets measured by one thing? Maybe it didn't change us as much as it revealed us." She looked at Tom.

"If either of us had given up hope, or stopped trying," Tom told her, "we wouldn't be here. You realize that. Not me on that cliff, or you when you thought Deke had killed me or in the Gauntlet. If either of us had given up we're not having this conversation."

Gail wrapped an arm around his waist. "If we didn't give up out here, why would we give up anywhere else?"

"We won't," Tom told her. "But what about Roarke? How does he ever get over this?"

"Same thing. We don't give up. We don't give up loving him. Exposing him to new things. Teaching him what we know. Telling him there are bad things and bad people in the world, but they don't make you who you are. I wish he hadn't seen what he did," Gail said, "at his age, *but he did*. . . . So you hope the old saw is true: that what doesn't kill you only makes you stronger. Same for us."

For a long moment they just listened to the sweet hush of the slow current.

"It's tamer down here than it was where we put in," Tom said.

"Yeah, rivers are like that," Gail said. "Marriages, too. You just have to buckle up for the rough spots."

Tom stuck both crutches under one arm and pulled Gail close against him. "I've been thinking about those basics you were talking about that first night on the river. Getting the shit kicked out of you is a good catalyst. Staring down a griz. Coming within a breath of drowning. Going through what we've gone through, we *should* be talking about them. They're so important.

"I know," Gail said softly. Her heart spilled over with renewed hope. She started to cry, to let the emotions flow out that she had kept in check for so long on the river—emotions she had to manage, she knew, to stay alive; but now she had to let go to begin the healing.

The river flowed and gurgled. Sun dappled its surface through the canopies of cottonwoods. Songbirds chirped. A trout rose and made a ring. Gail knew that in a river's life, this was old age for the River Wild—the slow, meandering part before it emptied itself into something bigger than it was—the Missouri, a few miles downstream. It was the same for people.

"There were northern lights last night," Tom said. "I saw them."

Gail peered at him, astonished. "No way."

"I could see them from my side of the river. They were so beautiful. They shimmied and danced and filled me up with faith and humility and a contentment I don't think I've ever felt before. They made me feel like I was part of something bigger than me, yet that embraced me. Isn't that what religion's supposed to do?"

"That's my understanding," Gail said.

Tom looked at her. "I think I joined your church last night."

Gail beamed. There was so much to say she knew to be true: that recognizing you were no more important in the scheme of things than a whitefish, or a leaf, or a river rock, was the most liberating thing—to acknowledge your insignificance, which in turn, empowered you as a part of a whole greater than the sum of its parts. Yet none of it was written down. There was no big book. No hocus pocus or hallowed days. Holy water, maybe. But you understood it by living it, by being part of it.

"Yeah," she confessed at the river's edge, "I like where they pass the collection plate."